Twisted Ruck

Ruck Boys
Book 3

Maggie Alabaster

Chapter One

Chelsea

A LONG, HARD SILENCE FOLLOWED MY WORDS.

"I could have sworn you just said Bruce Fergus is dead," Frost said. His usually tanned face was pale, green eyes troubled as he tried to absorb the words.

"That's what the article says." I couldn't bring myself to speak above a whisper. If I did, it might make this real.

I glanced back at my phone, but the words were still there on the screen. Sadie had sent me the link. She'd worked late the night before and didn't seem to be home yet. That wasn't unusual. Sometimes, she didn't get in until nine or ten o'clock. According to the timestamp, she sent me the message at five am.

"Let me look." Frost held out his hand for my

phone. He scanned the screen, lips slightly apart. "Fuck."

"Any time." Storm stepped out of my bedroom, looking sleepy and rubbing his face. He stopped in the doorway, taking us both in. "What is it? You look like the zombie apocalypse finally happened."

"There's no such thing as zombies." Dallas pushed past him and stepped into the kitchen. He wore only track pants and a sleepy face, like Storm.

He never got much sleep when he stayed at my place. Neither did I, to be honest, but I loved having them here. Especially last night. They helped me forget how Atlas walked away after our date.

Now, the memory flashed back into my mind, fresh as the moment it happened. Expression dark, he suggested he'd stop me from working with the Dusk Bay Smashers rugby team so he wouldn't have to see me anymore.

I thought I had thick skin, but it stung. It would for a while.

"What the hell is going on?" Storm demanded.

Frost handed the phone to him and leaned back against the countertop, his hands to either side of him.

"What the fuck?" Storm gaped at the screen. "This can't be right. Heart-attack?"

"People die of natural causes in Dusk Bay," I said absently. Once in a while.

All three of them stared at me for a couple of moments, like maybe I was out of my mind.

"They *do*," I argued. "That's all this is. As far as I know, he didn't have any enemies."

"But he might have," Dallas said. He glanced sideways at Frost.

Frost raised his hands. "Don't look at me. I didn't go anywhere near him. Anyway, I've been here all night."

"*Most* of the night," Dallas said.

"You've also been here for 'most of the night,'" Frost argued.

"Frost was with me before we got the call from Chelsea and headed over," Storm said. "And who says zombies aren't real?" He was clearly rattled by the news and trying to cover it with a hint of humour.

"I do, dumbass." Dallas tugged the fridge open and pulled out the bottle of milk. He poured himself a glass and drank it in a couple of gulps. "For the record, I haven't seen Bruce in a couple of days. I had nothing to do with it."

"Me either," I said. "The last time I spoke to him, it was amicable. What does this mean for the team?"

Frost stepped around behind me and lightly massaged my shoulders. "We'll get a new GM. Things will keep on keeping on."

"What does it mean for Chelsea working for the team?" Storm gave voice to the question I hadn't dared to ask.

"We should get to the stadium," Dallas said. "Coach will—"

Simultaneously, their phones beeped with incoming text messages.

"Call us in," Dallas finished. He pulled out his phone and checked the screen. "Bingo. Team meeting at ten."

"You guys should go," I said.

"Come with us," Frost said. "As far as I'm concerned, you're part of the team."

"I'm not really," I argued. "He didn't give me the job."

"Maybe he intended to but didn't get a chance," Frost suggested. It was an innocent suggestion, but my mind took it in a completely different direction.

My blood went cold. "I suppose that's possible."

Was this Atlas' doing? Somehow he knew Bruce was going to hire me, and got to him before he could? I wished I could rule that out, but the more I thought about it, the greater the chance I could rule it in.

"Atlas fucking Underwood," Storm growled. "If he killed Bruce to soothe his ego, I'm going to rip his arms off and beat him over the head with them."

Frost snorted a laugh. "I'm sorry, but I'd like to see that." He quickly added, "Only if Atlas was actually involved."

"I might do it anyway," Storm said. "He deserves it after treating Chelsea like shit."

"Don't go ripping arms off until you know what actually happened." I rubbed my temples with my thumb and the tips of my fingers. "Like I said, it might have been natural causes." Right now, that seemed as likely as the guys sprouting an extra cock each.

"I've waited this long," Storm said. "I can wait a bit longer." His jaw worked. At the same time, he curled his fingers into a fist and wrapped the other hand around it, like he was warming it up.

"I vote we get a place together after this," Frost said. He didn't elaborate, he just stepped back into the bedroom and started sorting through the clothes that lay scattered on the floor.

I stepped out of his track pants and offered them to him before I hurried in for a quick shower. I didn't want to turn up at the stadium messy and smelling of the three guys. Not today, anyway.

For once, none of them joined me. By the time I was dry and dressed, they were sitting around the table, drinking coffee and eating toast and fruit.

"We have breakfast for you." Dallas gestured to the seat beside him.

The moment I sat, he placed a hand on my leg. Whenever I was near, he had to touch me. Some women might have found it stifling, but I thought it was sweet. And that day, it was comforting. I liked to be touched. I liked knowing he cared about me so much.

"I'm not hungry," I admitted. In spite of that, I picked up a piece of toast and bit into the corner before washing it down with still-hot coffee. "I should be asking how you guys are doing. Bruce was a good GM. The team is going to feel his absence."

"Yeah," Storm agreed. "He was a good guy. One of the better ones. His wife and kids are going to be gutted."

"*I'm* gutted," Frost said. He pressed his lips together long enough for them to turn white. "Like Stormy said, he was a good guy. Whoever replaces him is going to have big boots to fill."

"Really big," Dallas agreed. "And they better hire Chelsea, or they might end up the same way." He nodded.

So far, he hadn't given me any indication he was into killing people, like Frost and my brother were. Maybe he was considering making an exception for anyone who got between me and my dream job. Or rather, got in the way of his ability to sneak off to the infirmary and fuck me once or twice a day.

Priorities.

"I was going to say that," Frost said.

"Can we *not* kill the new GM?" I said, finishing on a heavy sigh. "You don't even know who it'll be. They probably haven't had time to *start* considering a replacement."

The team would have to deal with today before they could think about tomorrow.

"I make no promises," Frost said. "But I'm willing to give them the benefit of the doubt. For now."

"You're starting to sound like my brother," I said with a sigh.

"Thank you." Frost grinned. "We could be a double act. Ice and Frost."

"Don't forget Storm," Storm said.

"The bad weather triplets," Dallas said dryly. "I'm starting to think I should change my name to Tornado. Might be a better nickname than Tex."

"Or Snow," Frost suggested. He snapped his fingers. "I know, Chelsea could be Snow. We could be Snow White and the Seven Smashers." He wiggled his eyebrows at the idea.

I shook my head in response. "I always preferred Rose Red."

What in the world would I do with seven guys? I had my hands full enough as it was. Not to mention all of my holes, a lot of the time.

"Like blood?" Frost asked.

"Like red roses," I replied firmly. "Red is my favourite colour."

It was also my brother's favourite colour, to the surprise of absolutely no one. He *did* choose it because it was the colour of blood. He also quite liked lavender, for no reason other than he liked the look of it.

"My favourite colour is the exact shade of your pussy," Dallas supplied.

"Mine too," Storm said.

"Mine is a tie between Chelsea's pussy and the colour of Storm's cock when he's hard," Frost said.

"I've always said you had good taste," Storm said, as he cupped his groin through his track pants. He smiled, but his stormy grey eyes remained troubled. His thoughts were on much more difficult topics than our favourite colours.

All of our minds should be.

This? It was our way of dealing with the situation. Joking around and talking about trivial things, rather than morbid ones.

"And I taste good," Frost said. He gulped down the last of his coffee and stood. "I don't know about you all, but I'm ready to get down there and face the music."

"Are you sure you're not guilty?" Dallas asked. "Because that's something a guilty person would say."

"I'm guilty of a lot of things," Frost agreed, "but having *anything* to do with Bruce dying isn't one of them."

He sighed out his nose after the last couple of words, his expression grim again. "I meant we'll have to face the fact it's true. You know what they say about not believing everything you read on the Internet."

"I don't think something like that would be up there if it wasn't true," Storm said reluctantly. "Let's head on in and find out for sure."

"And don't go pointing any fingers at Atlas until we have some idea whether or not he had anything to do with it," I said, giving them all a long look. "The police might be looking into the cause of death. We don't want to complicate things."

We shouldn't blame an innocent man for a

murder when no murder took place. If one had, I'd make sure the right people knew what happened. *The right people* being my brother. He'd either deal with Atlas directly, or he'd make sure the police found out what he did.

I pushed the thought to the side for now. I was getting way ahead of myself.

"I love that about you," Frost said. "He hurt you last night, but you're still not ready to hate on him." He leaned over and lightly kissed my mouth.

"It might mean I'm too naïve," I suggested.

And it might mean I spent a lifetime covering for criminals. A habit I wasn't going to break anytime soon, even if I wanted to. Those same people would have me killed if I got underfoot. My brother would try to stop them, but they'd persist until they got to me. He couldn't watch me twenty-four hours a day.

No, better to keep my mouth shut. It got me this far. I saw no reason to change now.

"It means you're a nicer person than Storm," Dallas said. "And me, before he starts throwing stones."

"Most people are nicer than us," Storm said with a shrug. He finished a piece of apple and got to his feet. "My SUV. I'll drive."

None of us was in the mood to argue with him. It

wasn't worth it at the best of times. Today was definitely *not* the best of times.

I couldn't shake the heavy feeling beginning to settle on me. Or the fear of facing Atlas. If he'd kill Bruce to keep me from working for the Smashers, then what else was he capable of? He might decide to go after Storm, Frost, or Dallas. Or he might decide I was an easier target.

If he killed me, my brother would go to war with him. Things would get very, very ugly very, very fast.

"Things will be okay." Frost laced his fingers in mine. "We'll get to the bottom of what happened. The team will get a new GM and you'll get the job. Everything can go back to normal."

I wasn't sure if that was possible. If Bruce didn't die of natural causes, then there was a nefarious reason for his death. If we didn't find it quickly, we would spend the rest of our lives looking over our shoulders, waiting for us to be next.

Chapter Two

Chelsea

We barely said a word on the way to the stadium. Everyone was lost in their thoughts, staring out the window as Dusk Bay rolled past.

I was so deep in my head, I didn't realise we arrived until we stopped in front of the security gate. The attendant opened it and waved us through, her expression as grim as ours.

"Looks like it's true," Frost said softly from the front seat beside Storm.

"Yeah," Storm said. "Looks like." He reversed the SUV into a parking space and killed the engine.

In silence, we climbed out of the vehicle and closed the doors behind us with four distinct thumps.

"Are you sure this is a good idea?" I stood beside

the SUV, my hand on the door handle. It might be better if I waited in the car.

"I can throw you over my shoulder and carry you in if you like," Storm suggested. He took a step towards me and lowered his shoulder as though he was about to do just that.

I held up my hands to ward him off. "I can walk. Nothing will raise eyebrows faster than you carrying me in there."

"In case you hadn't realised already, I don't give a shit about raising eyebrows," he said. But he straightened, grabbed my hand, tucked me to his side and headed towards the staff and players entrance.

"That's one thing we love about you," Frost said. "You give no shits. You go on being you and everyone else can get fucked."

Storm grunted. "That's me. No shits or fucks given. What you see is what you get."

Frost fell in on the other side of him and Dallas walked beside me, more or less surrounding me with a wall of muscle.

"Maybe we shouldn't hold hands," I said. "It might look like we're—"

"Together," Storm finished for me. "We are. You finished your practical training. I'm over here giving no more shits about what people think about us having a relationship with you. I'm not going to act like there's anything wrong with it, because there isn't."

"As soon as they know we're together, they'll start digging into my past," I argued. I was tempted to pull my hand out of his, turn tail and run.

He held me tight, not letting me draw back. "We'll deal with it. Come on. We're right there anyway."

He was right, we were too close to the door for me to bolt now. A handful of players and staff lingered just inside, and outside, talking amongst themselves in low voices. Their expressions all matched ours. Sad, confused and occasionally angry.

Most barely gave us a glance as we stepped through the open door, into a wide reception area that led to a bank of elevators.

Jay and Ramsey stood near the wall, watching us with guarded expressions. They silently appraised my body, like they always did, but nothing in their expressions indicated Atlas told them I used to work at Flirts. Not yet, anyway.

Jay's gaze lingered on me before turning to Frost and becoming colder. He was clearly still angry Frost kissed Atlas. Atlas hadn't said much about Jay during our date, so I had no idea where they stood with each other.

As for Ramsey, he was always a mystery to me. Doctor Stuart completed his physical, so I was yet to have a conversation with him. As far as I could tell, he didn't do conversations with anyone. I only heard him say one or two words at a time.

Not everyone was as open and warm as Frost, I supposed.

"Hello," I greeted them both. I saw no reason not to *try* to be friendly.

Jay's gaze dipped to where my hand was in Storm's. He rolled his lips a couple of times before looking back up. "Morning."

It wasn't the friendliest greeting, but it wasn't unfriendly either. He seemed to be wondering what the hell I saw in someone like Storm Keller.

He nodded to Dallas. "Tex."

"Jay." Dallas nodded in return. "Goat. S'up?"

Ramsey shrugged. "Same shit."

This was the first time I'd heard anyone call Ramsey by his nickname. I wondered if he lived up to it. He looked like he knew how to ram. I dropped my gaze to his groin for a few moments before forcing it back up to his face.

"Yeah." Dallas nodded again.

They conveyed a lot without saying much. It was a man thing, I supposed.

"Have any of you seen Atlas?" Jay squinted at me, but he seemed concerned, not accusing.

"Not since last night," I said. "We saw a concert and then...went separate ways. You haven't heard from him?"

"Nope," was Jay's simple response.

"I haven't seen him since training yesterday," Storm said. "Have you seen him, Frosty?"

"I was with you," Frost reminded him. "I haven't seen him either."

"Me either," Dallas said.

"Have you asked Goat?" Storm nodded towards Ramsey.

"Yeah," Ramsey said.

"He hasn't seen him either," Jay supplied. "I guess he'll...turn up."

"Like a bad smell, you won't get rid of him that easily," Storm said.

His indifferent expression suggested he'd be happy if Atlas never showed up at all. Or better yet, showed up floating face first in the bay, or in some kind of shallow grave. If that happened, he wouldn't lose any sleep over it.

I wasn't so sure about that. What if Bruce's death

had something to do with Atlas' absence? For all we knew, they could both be dead, killed by... I honestly couldn't begin to guess. Not unless one of the guys contacted my brother while I was asleep.

I glanced over at them, but was almost certain they hadn't done anything behind my back.

"He's not—" Jay shook his head. "Whatever. We should get to the team meeting."

"Coach Stanley likes to start on time," Frost said. "He'll be pissed off if we miss any of it." He seemed resigned, and in no hurry. As if maybe if we held off for a little while longer, it would turn out to be some kind of giant prank. One in very poor taste, but still better than the reality.

"Right," Storm agreed. He clasped my hand tighter before I could suggest I not attend the meeting. He really would throw me over his shoulder and carry me if I tried.

Honestly, I was curious what Coach Stanley had to say. And the rest of the team management. They all must be scrambling to keep the pieces of this puzzle together. I didn't envy them that task at a time like this. Between organising staff and dealing with the press, they'd have their hands full.

Of course, I was sad for Bruce and his family, but the timing couldn't have been worse. The team was days away from the first game of the season. Now was the time they needed everyone and everything in place, not up in the air like someone took a pack of cards and threw it into the bay.

Ramsey placed a hand on Jay's shoulder and they walked together, in front of us, to the meeting room.

Predictably, the place was packed with players and staff. They stood or sat in small groups, whispering and giving each other hugs. One of the older staff was handing out tissues to those who needed them. They might need another box or two before this day ended.

The only person who seemed to notice my presence was Doctor Stuart. He sat in a chair near the window, knees crossed. He looked weary, like he hadn't slept in a couple of days. He gave me a nod and a tight smile before turning his attention back to the front of the room.

I should have realised I could attend without ruffling feathers. No one was going to stop to check things like that today. Their minds were on more important things than me.

We shuffled to the back of the room and stood against the wall, where we could see and hear, but be out of the way.

"I hate these meetings," Frost muttered. "I always

want to say inappropriate things so only the people around me can hear them. That would be a shitty thing to do today."

"Yeah, today is a good day to keep it shut," Dallas agreed. He glanced down at the tired carpet on the floor. "I hate these things because it's fucking sad."

"Yes, it is," I said softly. The mood in the room was starting to get to me. A couple of people off to the side had tears sliding down their faces. I recognised one as Bruce's personal assistant. This must have hit her especially hard. Not as hard as his family, of course, but working close with someone and then losing them was tragic. Especially when Bruce's replacement might decide to replace her too.

I could definitely relate to that kind of uncertainty. I hoped for her sake she'd have her position sorted quickly.

I caught movement in the corner of my eye. When I looked around, it was to see Atlas step into the room, followed closely by head coach Max Stanley.

Before he could catch my eye, I looked away, vaguely aware that he moved to the corner. If anyone was going to cause an uproar over my presence here, it would be him.

Hopefully, he'd keep his peace until this was over.

I suspected he would. He seemed all too aware of the negative impact of making a scene in public. No, he'd wait and make a scene in private.

"Thank you all for being here today," Coach started. His words put an immediate end to the quiet talking around the room. "By now, you all know about the passing of Bruce Fergus. His wife found him in the early hours of the morning. She called an ambulance, but they were...too late."

He coughed, choking back emotion, fist over his mouth. For a while, he was unable to continue. I didn't know much about the relationship between Bruce and Coach Stanley, but it seemed there was a healthy dose of respect there.

Finally, he cleared his throat and continued.

"Because of this tragic circumstance, we find ourselves in a difficult position. A new general manager will be appointed as quickly as possible. A number of open positions were due to be filled in the next day or so. For now, those will be handed over to whoever is in charge of that area of operations. As far as I'm concerned, we continue to do as we've always done. Work hard and play hard. Bruce would want us to give everything we have to the coming season. I suggest we do that in his honour. When we hold that premiership cup up at the end of the season, we'll know we did it for him."

A rumble went through the meeting room, a subdued agreement to do as he suggested.

"That doesn't sound like a team ready to give it a red hot go," Coach said. He raised his hands and gestured around the room.

The players erupted in a chorus of shouts, claps and whistles.

"We've got this," Frost shouted out. "We can do this for Bruce!"

"For Bruce!" someone echoed.

"For Bruce!" the whole room said in unison.

I actually caught Storm quickly wiping his eyes. I leaned into him and squeezed his hand.

"I'm not crying, you are," he told me.

I sniffed. "I'm only crying a little bit." I dabbed at my own eyes before catching Doctor Stuart looking at me again. One of his eyebrows rose. Did that mean what I thought it meant? If he was allowed to choose his staff, did he choose me?

I managed a faint, hopeful smile, which faded slightly when Atlas stepped into my line of sight.

He was also looking at Doctor Stuart, but rather than looking angry, he looked triumphant.

Chapter Three

Chelsea

"This is... Um... Quite the turn of events." Doctor Stuart placed his phone down on his desk and turned to face me. If I thought he looked weary at the meeting, he looked downright exhausted now. "I can't help feeling personally responsible."

"Why on earth would you feel like that?" I closed the door behind us and stood leaning against it.

"He was due for a medical," Doctor Stuart said. "I kept reminding him and he kept putting me off. I should have insisted. If I had, I might have found any issues long before they got out of hand."

"If Bruce was anything like the other guys around here, he was as stubborn as a granite boulder," I said. "Convincing him to take the time would have been near impossible."

Doctor Stuart scrubbed a hand over his face. "It was, but I should have pushed my weight around and made him come here."

"I'm sure you tried." I stepped further into the room. "How many times did he cancel appointments with you?" I was guessing, but it was probably a pretty good guess. Men like Bruce knew how to be busy when they wanted to avoid something.

"Three or four," Doctor Stuart admitted. "Something was always more pressing. Scheduling, or the salary cap. Or somebody forgot to book flights to next month's games. *Something*. He always said he'd get around to it when the season started. And now...he can't." He swallowed heavily, struggling to contain his emotions.

I wanted to tell him I suspected Bruce's death wasn't from natural causes. Before I could confront Atlas, he'd got sent off with the rest of the team to train. I needed to speak to him, and soon, but this had to come first.

"It's not your fault," I said. "You could have given him a dozen medicals and this might have happened anyway." Chances were, it would have. What had Atlas done to him? And why? What might he do to Doctor Stuart if he made the choice to hire me? If Atlas thought he was going to lay a finger on the team doctor, he'd have to go through me. Doctor Stuart was a good man, he didn't deserve to be killed, especially because of me.

"That will be up to the coroner to determine," Doctor Stuart said.

I forced back a grimace. If my brother did the autopsy, the official findings wouldn't show Bruce was murdered. Not if Atlas was involved.

I'd talk to him and make sure he determined the GM's cause of death was something Doctor Stuart couldn't have found with a regular medical. Nothing medically preventable.

"Right," I said simply. "This is such a sad time for the team."

"It is," he agreed. "But let's not spend too much time on self-pity. Bruce and I had an appointment for this morning to discuss the position here. If he made a decision, he didn't tell me. As well as one other physician, I'd like to officially offer you the position with the team. You'll be the junior for a while, but I suspect you'll be doing my job in a few years." He gave me a watery smile and held out his hand.

I should have been excited, but Bruce's death took the shine off somewhat. Still, I took Doctor Stuart's hand and shook it.

"Thank you so much. I promise I won't let you down."

"I know you won't," he said. "I expect you to hit the ground running. Bruce informed Doctor Otis Skinner of his appointment yesterday. Between the three of us, we'll have this place shipshape. Doctor Skinner has lots of experience working with professional athletes."

I frowned briefly. "Didn't he work for the Sydney Devils?"

"He did, but he was looking for a change of scenery." Doctor Stuart pulled his chair out from behind his desk and sank into it. "He's been doing a lot of research in aqua therapy and wants to put it into practice here."

The stadium had a state-of-the-art pool for the players to use while recovering from injuries. The pressure on muscles, bones and ligaments was less in water than it was on land, supporting healing while minimising the risk of further injury. Aqua therapy was nothing new, but I was fascinated to discuss his research when he arrived. I'd always been a geek for learning new things.

"I look forward to meeting him," I said. "I really appreciate this opportunity. This is going to be amazing." For the first time, I let myself become excited.

"It'll certainly be interesting," Doctor Stuart agreed. "If a little turbulent for a while."

"Who do you think they'll choose to replace Bruce?" I asked.

Doctor Stuart leaned his elbows on the desk and clasped his hands. "My pick would be Dominic King. He's more than ready for a position like that. He's been a manager for the Sydney Devils for the last few years."

"It sounds like we're poaching all their best people," I said. I knew of King, but I never met the man. From what I heard, he was a good choice.

Doctor Stuart smiled. "It does, doesn't it? I can't say I have any regrets about that. They may even teach us a thing or two."

I scoffed playfully. "They'll learn a lot here."

"That too," Doctor Stuart agreed. "I think we'll learn a lot from each other. We have complimentary skills and experience between all of us. Best of all, we have passion for the game, and taking care of the players."

"That we do," I said.

I had lots of passion for at least three in particular. And, in spite of our date, I was still attracted to Atlas. Cautiously so. I wasn't going to jump in too deep, not until I knew what the hell he was up to.

After my brief conversation with Jay and Ramsey, I got the impression Atlas and Jay were a package deal. Atlas may not realise it yet, but Jay definitely had.

I didn't want to interfere with their relationship, but that was something they'd have to work out between them. Atlas may not feel the same way about the other player. And if he did? That was something we'd deal with later.

Then there was Ramsey, who fascinated me, although I wasn't entirely sure why. Maybe because he was such a closed book, I was curious to tease the pages open.

"I trust you have a passport," Doctor Stuart said, breaking through my thoughts.

"Recently updated and ready to go," I said with a smile.

"Good, because you'll be doing a lot of travel with the team," he said. "Primarily, over the ditch." He jerked his head towards the bay, indicating roughly in the direction of New Zealand.

"I can't wait," I said. "I love to travel."

"They all say that to start with." He gave me a wry smile. "Give it a year or two and you'll be sick of the inside of aircraft and airports. And hotel lobbies. The guys will tell you the travel is the best and worst part of playing. Between games, they often spend a lot of time waiting. Waiting for buses, waiting for planes. It can be tedious at best."

"I still can't wait," I said. I suspected things wouldn't get boring with Storm, Frost and Dallas, as well as the other guys.

"Remember what we said about being discreet," Doctor Stuart said. "It won't go unnoticed if you join the mile high club on a team flight."

My face heated. "I wouldn't dream of it." Without doubt, the guys would, but something like that would be more likely to get me fired than having a relationship with them in the first place.

"I'm sure." He nodded slowly. "You'll have a bunch of paperwork to fill out before you start. Tax forms and whatnot. The usual required bullshit. And you'll need a new identification pass and entry card. And a few of the official team shirts for press conferences and things like that. You may need to attend those occasionally. You'll also be put on the roster for the family clinic. Don't expect to get the best hours. The new doctors always get the worst shifts." He was not sugarcoating things.

I smiled. "I wouldn't have expected anything less. I'll work my way up until someone else is getting those." I didn't care what shifts I got, as long as I got shifts. As it was, I was used to working all sorts of late and long hours. Working without stilettos would be a welcome change. And with my clothes on.

Doctor Stuart nodded and let out a long sigh. "I wish Bruce was here to welcome you officially, but you're stuck with me."

"I don't consider myself *stuck*," I said. "It's been an honour training under you. I look forward to working with you. And learning from you." With all his years of experience, I'd be stupid not to watch closely and absorb everything.

"You say that now, but give it a year." He sat back in his chair and rubbed his neck. "You might feel differently then."

"Are you trying to put me off accepting the position?" I asked. "Because I'm still in."

I was *so* in. My inner little girl was itching to jump up and down and scream. She chose this path for herself a long time ago and now she was finally there. She was ecstatic.

"I didn't peg you for the running away kind," he said. "If you were, you'd have done that after the first day here. Or the first week. Others have before you. But you didn't. Everything that's been thrown at you, you've taken it in stride. Not that I expected anything less from Doctor Isaac Miller's sister. You both have ambition to spare. You in particular."

He was clearly impressed. If he knew what my brother was really like, I couldn't tell. All I got was a sense of professional, mutual admiration between two doctors.

What would he think if he knew? I had a feeling it took a lot to surprise Doctor Stuart. Even something like that.

"Yes, we do," I agreed. "We were raised to go after what we wanted, and we do. I don't think either of us has ever backed down from a challenge."

"That's good to hear, because this job will challenge you," Doctor Stuart said. "It will challenge you in ways you haven't dreamt of yet." He unclasped his hands and pressed them together, lining up his fingertips as though doing so was momentarily fascinating. "I have a feeling you're going to enjoy it."

"I intend to enjoy every moment of it," I assured him. "I know how privileged we are to work here. I'm not going to take that for granted for a second."

But I was going to get to the bottom of whatever the hell Atlas pulled. If he'd tried to keep me from getting this job, that was too fucking bad. I wasn't letting it go without one hell of a fight.

"Of course you're not," Doctor Stuart agreed. "If I

thought you would, I would have passed you over for the other candidates. To be honest, your appointment here will raise an eyebrow or two. We had some very experienced doctors apply, but the team has had enough turmoil already. The players know you and I know how you work. That's why I'm offering it to you. That's why I gave my recommendation to Bruce."

"Do you think he would have hired me?" I asked.

Did I really want to know the answer to that question? I wasn't entirely sure, but now I'd asked, I might as well listen to the response. Even if it was something I didn't want to hear.

Doctor Stuart hesitated before shaking his head. "If he knew what was good for him, he would have, but I don't know. Otis Skinner was the only one we discussed and settled on. I'm sorry I can't give you a better answer than that."

"That's okay," I said. I had a feeling I knew who could.

Chapter Four

Chelsea

I thought hunting down Atlas might be difficult. Training was done and he might have gone home. Or to...I didn't know where.

Instead, he was waiting for me when I stepped out of the infirmary. Leaning against the wall, arms and ankles crossed. His brown-gold eyes watched me draw closer until I stopped in front of him.

"What did you do?" I asked. I wasn't in the mood to mince words. Not after our date.

He smirked. "What do you *think* I did?" He looked impressed with himself. Okay, more impressed with himself than usual.

I was about to respond when a couple of the team's staff walked past. I waited until they were gone. "We should take this somewhere else."

He slid me a sly glance. "Whatever you say." He gestured toward a side room.

I was starting to see why Storm wanted to punch him. I was tempted to do it myself. While wanting to tear his clothes off and fuck his brains out. Conflicting thoughts for sure.

I stepped into the storage room and stood to the side as he closed the door behind us. "Well?" I placed my hands on my hips.

"I'm very well," he said, his smug mask not slipping. "And you're very welcome. I assume Doctor Stuart hired you?"

"Yes, he did," I said carefully.

I thought that would piss him off, but if anything, he seemed pleased. Smugly so. "Which brings me back to 'what did you do'?"

"I think we were at me asking you what you thought you knew." He leaned against the door and raised his eyebrows at me.

"Did you have anything to do with Bruce Fergus' death?" I asked bluntly.

"Define 'anything,'" he said evasively.

I rolled my eyes at him. "Did. You. Kill. Bruce. Fergus?"

"I might have," he said. Still completely unperturbed.

"Why?" I demanded. "Last night you said you didn't want me working here. I got the impression you'd do anything to make sure that didn't happen."

He shrugged one shoulder. "I had a change of heart. I thought about it for a while and realised you were right. You being a stripper in a past life isn't a big deal. It's not a dealbreaker. I want you and I want you *here*."

"So why—" I shook my head. "How would killing him have achieved that?" I tried, but none of this was making sense.

"He wasn't going to hire you," Atlas said. "I went to talk to him. To ask what his plans were. He said you didn't have enough experience. Not as a doctor."

"What does that mean?" My heart sank a little.

"It means someone told him what you used to do, and he decided it wasn't in the team's best interest to put you in a position here. I suggested he change his mind. He declined." His eyes flashed with a brief moment of fury.

"So you did... What? I know he wasn't beaten to death." That wouldn't have gone unnoticed by the police.

"I was nice enough to bring him a beer when I dropped by," Atlas said. "We drank while we had a nice chat. When it became obvious he wasn't going to listen to reason, I added something to his."

"You poisoned him," I said. I closed my eyes, trying to get my head around that. "You poisoned him to make sure I got the job here."

"Yep," Atlas said. "And to make sure he didn't share what he knew with anyone else."

"Did he say how he knew?" I asked. My pulse raced faster. Who was out there telling people about my past? And why?

"We didn't quite get to that point," Atlas admitted. "He started feeling unwell and headed off to bed. I went back to my place and stayed there until I got the message from Coach this morning."

"You didn't go to Hazards." After the concert, two fans approached him and invited him to the bar there. After he walked away from me, I'd assumed he followed them there. The idea of him touching those women made me want to slip something into *their* drinks.

Was this how Jay felt when Frost kissed Atlas? I assumed so.

"I thought about it," he said. "Then I realised something." He pushed himself off the door and stepped closer to me. "It's you I want. Not a quick fuck with some random chicks."

He ran the pad of his thumb down my cheek. Barely touching. Just enough to feel the calluses on his skin.

"What about Jay?" I asked softly. "I know he cares about you."

"I care about him." Atlas' hand dropped to my shoulder. "In a perfect world, I'd be with both of you."

"How does he feel about that?" Better we have this conversation now, rather than destroying his friendship with the scrum-half.

"I dunno." Atlas half-closed his eyes. "We haven't talked about it. It's not an easy thing to talk about, you know? What do I say? 'I know you barely know her, but let's all get involved?' You two might hate each other."

"You're right, it's not easy," I agreed. "It's already difficult with you and Storm always at each other's throats. Throw Jay into that and it's rucking messy."

"It's very rucking messy," Atlas agreed. He lowered his forehead to mine. "But if we want it enough, we'll make it work, right?"

"Exactly," I whispered. "You should talk to Jay before this goes further. Figure things out. I'll talk to the others and make sure they aren't plotting your grisly demise."

He chuckled. "They probably are anyway, knowing those guys."

"I don't think Frost is," I said. "I think he likes you too. And Dallas has been telling them to lay off you, so you might also have a supporter there."

"Frosty and Tex have good taste," Atlas said. "So does Jay. Storm might too, for all I know, but he's too busy with his head up his ass."

"You're tight with Ferris Ramsey too, aren't you?" I asked, trying to keep my tone casual.

Atlas lifted his head and regarded me with curious eyes. "Kinda. He's the only guy on the team who made us feel welcome. Everyone else treats Jay and I like we have the plague."

"I'm sorry," I said softly. "You might have more familiar faces coming soon." I told him about Otis Skinner, and Doctor Stuart's speculation that Dominic King might be the new GM.

"Interesting," Atlas said slowly. "Former Devils might take over here." He seemed to like the idea.

"We're all Smashers here," I scolded lightly.

He smiled. "That's appropriate, because I want to smash you." One hand on my hip, he lowered his mouth to mine, kissing me gently at first before diving in deeper, like he might devour me.

I put my hands on his waist, feeling his firm

warmth under the fabric of his T-shirt. I worked my way underneath it, running my palms up and down his sculpted abs and over his flat stomach.

At the same time, my lips and tongue explored his, tasting a hint of coffee in his mouth. I groaned as his other hand wandered up my body, the heel of his hand sliding over my nipple, making it pebble.

He kissed the side of my mouth and trailed kisses down my cheek, to my neck. Lightly, he grazed his teeth over my skin before biting down on my shoulder.

The sudden jolt of delicious pain sent a shiver all the way through my body. I whispered, "Atlas."

"You're so fucking beautiful." He bit me again, this time lower down. "Fucking tasty too. I bet anything your pussy tastes like heaven." He ran the tip of his tongue over where he bit before lowering himself to his knees and pushing my skirt up. He grabbed the front of my panties and tore them, leaving the lacy fabric in shreds.

"When do you start working here?" He looked up at me. "Officially."

"The day after tomorrow," I said breathlessly.

"Good, I'm going to tear your panties off then too, first thing in the morning, so you can walk around all day without them." He grabbed my leg and draped it over his shoulder before diving in deeper, his tongue raking over my already wet pussy.

I moaned, mostly from his expert touch, but partly at the idea of working while commando. The guys would love that, especially Dallas. One less piece of fabric between me and their cocks.

"I was right," Atlas said between licks. "So tasty."

"So good," I whispered. I ran my fingers through his hair, while watching him flick his tongue over and around my clit. He slid a couple of fingers inside me and curled around to start stroking my insides.

"Come for me, Chelsea," he said. "I want to hear how you sound when you come."

I groaned again. "I'm so close. Don't stop." Every time he lapped his tongue over me, he touched my piercing as well as my clit, making them come together and drive me crazy.

He didn't stop. He went on licking and stroking until I shattered into too many pieces to count. My vision went dark, broken only by the flare of fireworks that sounded a lot like the roar of blood. Nothing in any universe existed at that moment but absolute pleasure.

He didn't stop until I came all the way down from my orgasm and slumped against the wall, trying to catch my breath. He circled my insides with his fingers a couple of times before pulling them out and rising to his feet. He pressed them between my lips. "Taste yourself," he whispered. "See how delicious you are."

I opened my mouth and sucked on his fingers, tasting salt and tang. I hummed my appreciation. "So good."

"Very good." He pulled his fingers out and kissed me. "For the record, the sound of you coming is even better than Ice Blue Roses."

"With a smaller audience," I said.

He snorted softly. "This time. When the other guys fuck you, do they do it in front of each other?"

"Yes, they do," I said. "In front of each other and *with* each other."

"They'll want to watch us?" It seemed more of a statement than a question.

"Watch, participate," I agreed. "They're getting very open with each other. If you and I are involved, they'll want to get open with you too. Is that something you want?"

He only hesitated for a moment before simultaneously nodding and shrugging. "If that's what it means to be with you, then I'm in. I'm not shy, no reason to start now. Although..." He cocked his head.

"What?" I prompted.

"If Storm is going to give a running commentary or critique on my methods, I'm going to knock his block off."

I laughed. "I'm sure he'll be able to contain himself. I think he's going to be too busy taking part to bother criticising your skills. Who knows, you might enjoy each other some day."

A hint of pink crept up Atlas' cheeks. "Is this one of those 'he must like you, because he's being a prick to you,' things?"

"I hadn't thought about that, but it might be." Now I desperately wanted to see Storm and Atlas kiss each other.

"Huh. We'll see, I guess." He smoothed down the side of my skirt. "I want to fuck you, but you're right. I should speak to Jay first. Otherwise, I feel like I'd be cheating. Even though we haven't really talked about...you know, us."

I pushed away the bubble of disappointment. I wanted to feel his cock inside me, but this was about more than sex. Everyone had to be on board with this, or it could blow up in all our faces.

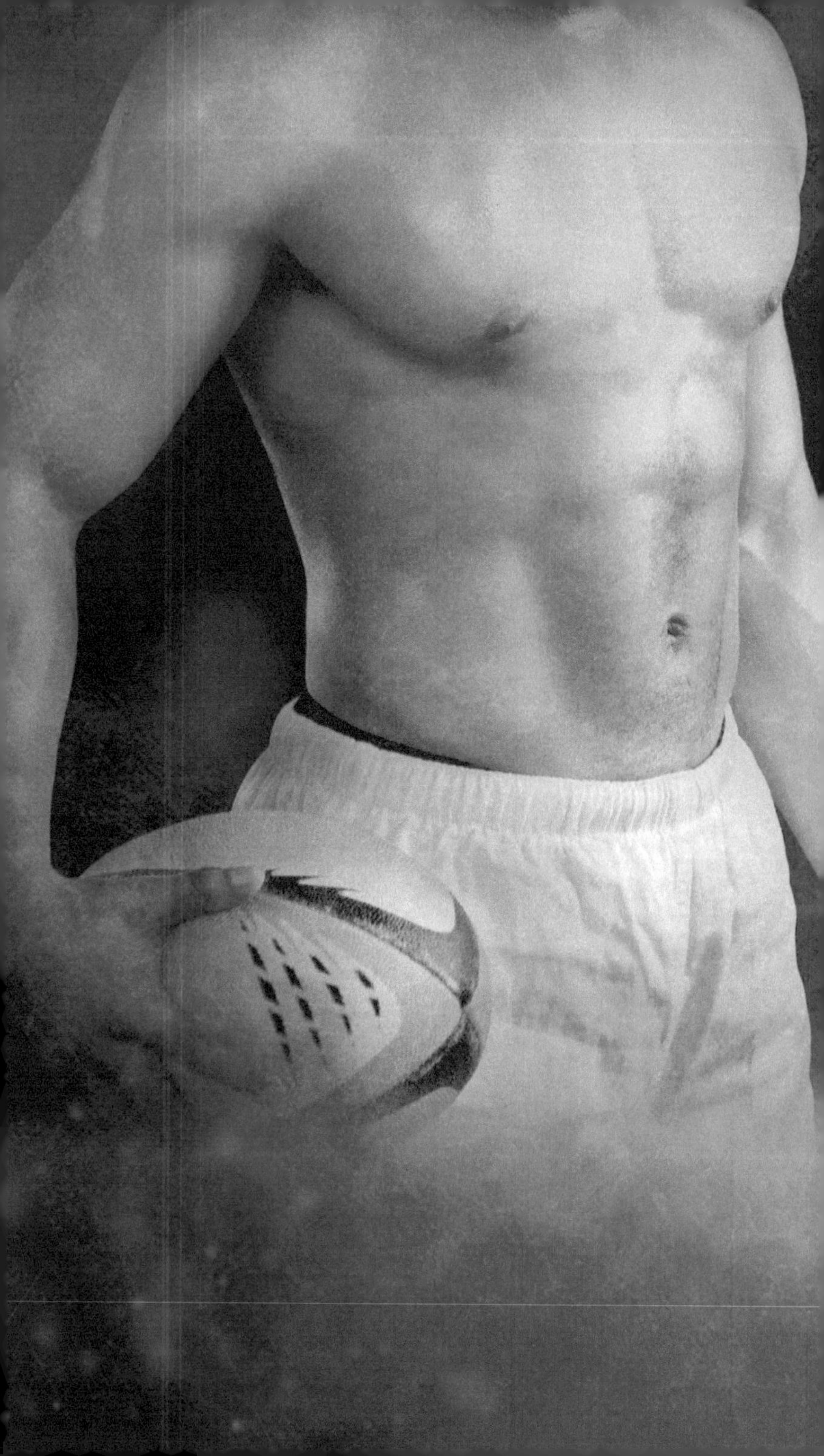

Chapter Five

Dallas

I grunted. "I respected Bruce, but now I don't know what to think."

I ate my sandwich with one hand, the other on Chelsea's thigh, my fingers between them. My favourite place for any of my body parts to be. Between her beautiful legs.

I still wanted to kick my own ass for responding to her the way I did the first time she sucked me off. I ran out the door like a dumb prick.

As soon as I slammed said door behind me, I realised I should have stayed. Pride kept me from going back into the room. Or maybe it was stupidity.

Either way, I went back for more later and didn't regret a moment of it. When I was near her, I couldn't regret it anyway. My brain was barely coherent. All I could focus on was her. Occasionally, the conversation going on around us. She was a whirlpool, and I was a piece of flotsam, twisting and turning my way around her, never breaking loose. Never wanting to break loose.

"You should still respect Bruce," Chelsea said. "He had a point, I don't have the experience. I might not be what the team needs."

"You're what I need," I said. "And if he didn't realise the team needed you, he is...was, out of his mind." I stroked my thumb up and down her warm skin.

"What I want to know is, who told him about your past?" Storm growled. "Fucker can end up the way Bruce did, far as I'm concerned."

"I have no idea who would have told him," Chelsea said. "Unless..." She frowned.

Storm turned around and frowned at her. "Unless what? Unless Atlas was bullshitting, and Bruce didn't know? Unless he was the one who told him?"

"Unless Atlas told Jay, and Jay told Bruce," Frost said. "Jay might have done what he thought Atlas wanted. Chelsea away from the team. He might have thought he was doing Atlas a favour."

"Joke's on him," I said softly.

"Right," Chelsea said. "I got the impression Jay didn't know, but I could be wrong. Fuck knows I've been wrong before. If that was what happened... Atlas was going to talk to Jay." She winced. "That might not go well. Atlas is going to be pissed off."

"Serves Jay right if he did," Storm said. He pulled out a chair, turned it around and straddled it. "Atlas might save us the hassle of having to get rid of him."

"No killing your teammates." Chelsea stared him down. "I'll make sure Atlas doesn't either. If I knew what he planned to do to Bruce, I would have stopped him." She ended the sentence with a regretful sigh.

"Then you wouldn't be working with us." I crept my hand up higher. "We might not see you every day. We would have been travelling without you." If I didn't put my cock in her at least once or twice a day, my balls would explode. That was how it felt, okay? I'd had nights without her at the insistence of the other guys, but I hadn't liked a moment of it.

"Which brings us back to moving in together," Storm said. "My place." Like usual, he left no room for argument.

"I like my place," I argued anyway.

"My place is bigger." His jaw worked back and forth, that stubborn look in his eyes. "And it's safer."

"Didn't someone almost get shot while they were looking out the window of Powell Tower?" I asked.

"*Almost* being the key word," Storm said. "You can't shoot someone through bullet-proof glass."

"Pretty sure you can," I said.

"They didn't," Storm snapped. "And they won't. There's nowhere safer in Dusk Bay."

"What about the mansions on the cliff?" Frost asked. He raised his hands when Storm shot him a look. "Just asking."

"At least one of those has come under attack in the past," Chelsea said softly. "If people want to get in, they will."

I wanted to get in. I wanted it very much. I ran my thumb over the gusset of her panties. Smiled when she shivered.

"Like I said, my place is safer," Storm insisted. "There's enough bedrooms and bathrooms for everyone."

No sooner had he said those words than I said, "I'm sharing with Chelsea."

"I was going to say that." Frost gave me the side eye.

Storm eyed us both. "There's room for one of those beds that fit ten people if we need it."

"That would work." Frost grinned. "Room for Chelsea and nine guys."

It was Chelsea's turn to eye him. "Or plenty of room for me to sleep spread out."

"As long as I'm there, I don't care," I said. "My cousin has a removal truck. I'll call him later."

"Do I get a say in this?" Chelsea asked, her tone dry, but not pissed off. She knew this was happening and she was rolling with it. Good girl.

"No," Storm told her. "I told you a long time ago you were moving in with me at some point. This is that point. The sooner we get it done, the better."

I slipped a finger under her panties and over her damp pussy. "It's for the best. We can keep all of our stuff and ourselves in one place. When we're travelling, we don't have to worry about people breaking into four places."

"Or even one," Storm said. "No one breaks into Powell Tower."

Chelsea's breath came a little faster as I rubbed my thumb over her clit. She was trying to keep her expression neutral, so the rest of the cafeteria wouldn't know what was happening under the table.

"Storm can't get enough of our company," Frost said. That clearly went both ways.

"How long before Atlas moves in too?" I rubbed

harder as she subtly rolled her hips, grinding her pussy against my thumb.

"That might be a bit too soon," she said. Her eyes were half-closed, lips apart, enjoying the way I touched her.

"We might need to look at one of those mansions after all," Frost said. "I heard there's one on the market right now. Something about it having six or seven bedrooms and bathrooms. We could have one each. And room for guests."

Storm scowled.

"Wouldn't hurt to take a look," I said without glancing in his direction.

Right now, my eyes were on Chelsea's chest, and the way her breasts rose and fell with each breath. She was close to coming, right here in the stadium cafeteria. I was harder than hell. I should take her away from here and fuck her, but I was fascinated that she was letting me do this here.

She loved sex and she loved experimenting with it. As far as I could tell, she hadn't found anything she didn't enjoy, including having my cock inside her all night. She never once tried to put me off, or claim she had enough. Whenever I needed her, she was ready for me.

She was the most perfect woman I ever met.

Beautiful, smart and sexy as hell. And the sound she made when she came was amazing.

That very sound slipped between her lips as she ground harder. All three of us watched her with eager eyes as she came on my hand. My thumb was drenched with her release. Her panties must've been saturated. And no one at any of the nearby tables knew a thing.

"You're incredible," I said. It wouldn't go unnoticed if I bent her over the table and fucked her, otherwise I would. All three of us would. Was that something Atlas would do?

The thought had me curious and even more aroused. Chelsea deserved all the cock she could handle. Which, so far, was a lot.

She blinked a couple of times, trying to clear her vision. "If anyone saw—" Her cheeks were adorably pink with a post-orgasmic glow and a hint of embarrassment.

Not that she had anything to be embarrassed about. I could never understand why people got so secretive about sex in the first place. If I had my way, we'd fuck like monkeys anywhere and everywhere the mood took us. Wouldn't it be healthier than hiding something so natural behind closed doors?

"No one saw," Frost assured her. "No one but us."

He glanced around, double checking once again. This wasn't something he wanted to be wrong about. The last thing we needed was for Chelsea to lose her job since she finally had it.

I pulled my fingers away and locked my eyes on her while I licked them clean. Then I proceeded to finish my sandwich, which wasn't as tasty as her release.

"Lucky for them. I'd have to poke their eyes out," Storm said in a growl. "Here's what we need to do. Tex, call your cousin. Get him sorted out as quickly as possible." He nodded to me.

"Frosty, if you feel like looking into that mansion, go for it. It can't hurt to look, and we might need it someday. We also need to find out who the fuck told Bruce about Chelsea."

"I'll talk to Atlas again," she said. "Once he's spoken to Jay."

"Dinner at my place," Storm said. "Invite him. We'll figure it out then." After a moment he added, "Invite Jay too, if he wants to come. Sounds like if we get one, we get both."

He looked like he'd prefer to chew rocks than be involved with either of them, but like the rest of us, he was invested in Chelsea. He'd put up with them if it meant being with her if that was what she wanted.

If it wasn't, he'd waste no time in telling them to fuck off. Neither would I. I didn't want anyone hanging around unless she wanted them to.

There was nothing any of us wouldn't do for her, to make her happy. Whether it meant giving her orgasms or putting up with people we butted heads with. We'd do all of it. Anything she asked. Anything she hinted at.

Bruce wasn't the first person one of us killed. It wasn't the top of my bucket list, but if I had to, I'd kill for her. Hell, I'd die for her. The woman was everything and more.

"I think I should talk to them separately first," Chelsea said slowly. "If you're there, they're going to be on the defensive. Let me hear what they have to say, then you guys can be involved."

"Atlas killed Bruce," Storm reminded her. "I don't like the idea of you being alone with him."

"He's not going to do anything to me," she said. "He's not going to kill me, at least."

"You're going to fuck him," Storm stated.

"I might," she replied easily. "But you already knew that would happen sooner or later."

We did know. It was only a matter of time before they were together. Another cock to add to her collection. As many as she needed, I'd be happy for her. If a little jealous and my balls a little blue.

Storm grunted. "What about Jay?"

"I'll see what happens when we're together," she said. "He might not want me."

"He's not that dumb," Storm said. He looked like he might argue further, but finally he nodded. "You're right, they won't open up to you if I'm there. Figure things out. And start packing." He nodded to end the conversation.

Frost already had his phone out. "It might sound weird, but I like house hunting. It's fun when you have money to actually buy property." His green eyes scanned back and forth as he read his screen.

I grunted my agreement. Rugby did a lot for me, including filling my bank account to a level I wouldn't have dreamt of. I never would have imagined I could afford a house overlooking the ocean in Dusk Bay. It was wild.

Of course, I made sure my parents were comfortable first. They deserved it after everything they did for me. Encouraging me to play footy and driving me to all the games and all the training sessions. Shivering on the sidelines while I played. Giving back to them was one of the best things I ever did. I couldn't wait to introduce them to Chelsea. They'd love her as much as I did.

"I'll call Marty," I said. "Make sure he can fit us in in the next couple of days." If not, I'd buy a truck and find people to help us load and offload. It wasn't as though we didn't know a team full of strong, fit guys more than willing to help. I helped several of them move house in the past. They'd pitch in and return the favour.

"Let's do this." Storm looked smug, like he did when he got his way. Since that was most of the time, he spent a large portion of the day looking smug.

Lucky for him I wasn't going to fight him on this. I liked my place, but I liked being with Chelsea more. If I was honest, I'd gotten used to the guys' company too. We'd quickly become something of a family to each other. One that centred around the most beautiful woman on the face of planet Earth.

I pulled out my phone and tapped on the screen before putting the device to my ear.

"Hey, cuz, I need a favour."

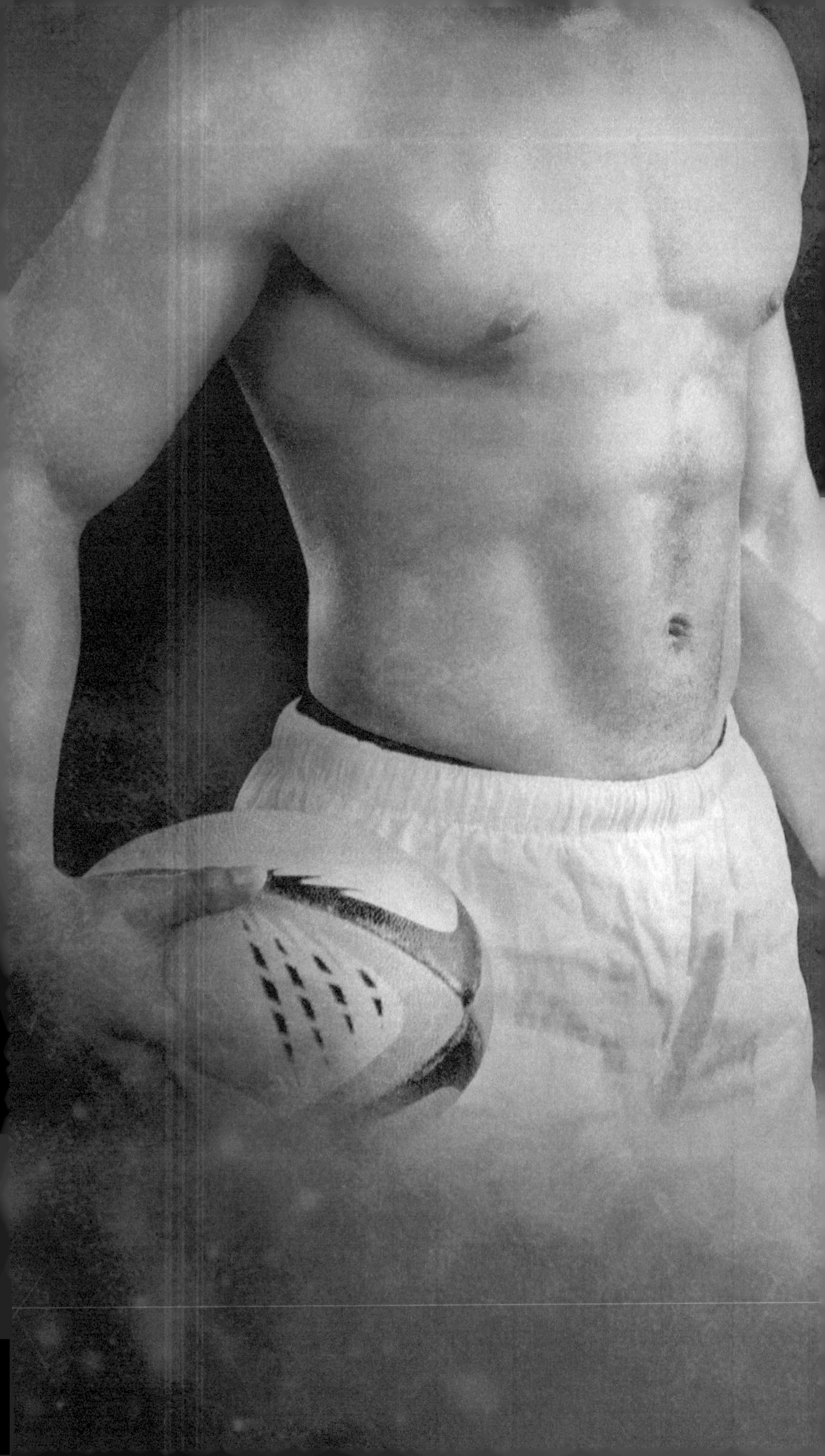

Chapter Six

Chelsea

"Hey, thanks for coming." I stepped back, opening the door wider so Atlas and Jay could enter.

Atlas gave me a kiss on the cheek.

Jay gave me a long look before walking past. "Doc," he said with a grunt.

"Jay." I shut the door behind them. "How's things?"

"Complicated," Jay said. He stopped to glance down at the pile of packing boxes in the kitchen. "You're really moving in with Storm."

"Yes." I picked up the boxes on the way home and got started while I waited for them to arrive for dinner. "It'll save me a fortune in rent."

"That's the only good reason I can think of to live

with Storm Keller." Atlas stood beside Jay, his elbow on the scrum-half's shoulder.

"He's not so bad when you get to know him," I said. "I'm sorry he didn't give you a chance to do that yet. He's...stubborn."

"That's one word for it," Jay said.

"Why don't you boys sit and I'll get dinner onto plates?" I picked up the box that sat on the top of the table and placed it aside.

While they got comfortable, I spooned risotto into bowls and placed them in front of the guys, and one for myself.

"So, you two talked," I said. I stabbed a piece of mushroom with my fork and pushed it into my mouth.

"Atlas told me he killed Bruce for you," Jay said. Clearly he wasn't going to spare any words.

"I didn't ask him to," I said, more defensive than I intended.

"You wouldn't have had to." Jay glanced over to Atlas. "He made up his own mind, like he always does, and did what he wants." He didn't seem to mean it in a negative way. Rather that Atlas took care of people he cared about, whether they liked it or not.

Atlas shrugged. "Bruce didn't give me much

choice in the end. I gave him the chance to change his mind and he didn't take it. That's on him." He also kept his words concise, not mentioning my past. Not even alluding to it. His expression suggested I shouldn't say anything about it. Not right now.

I gave him a faint nod to show I understood, but nothing more than that. We'd deal with it when the time came. In the meantime, Jay spoke like he hadn't noticed a thing.

"Atlas is a Scorpio," Jay said. "Once you have his loyalty, you're stuck with him for life." The look he gave the lock clearly said he wasn't going anywhere either. "This is good risotto."

"Thanks," I said. We ate in silence for a few moments before I got down to the reason they were here. "Both of you care about each other, don't you? A lot." My gaze shifted from one to the other and back again. "I don't want to get between you."

"Yes, you do," Jay said.

I was about to protest, but realised what he was actually implying.

I snorted a soft laugh. "I meant I don't want to damage your relationship with each other." I definitely wouldn't mind being in the middle of the two players. I was only human after all.

"What is that anyway? Are you friends, or are you more?"

"More." Jay shrugged without slowing down his eating. "He's not leaving me for you."

"I didn't expect him to," I said. I glanced over to Atlas, trying to figure out his thoughts. He seemed to be focused on eating, but I knew he was following the conversation. Maybe waiting to see where it would end up.

"What do you expect?" Jay asked. "Am I supposed to fall head over heels for you too?"

I regarded him for a few moments. "I'm starting to think you believe I'm some kind of princess who's gathering a horde of men around her." I paused for a beat before adding, "Dragon might be a better analogy."

"Aren't you?" he asked. "You have three boyfriends already, what do you want with Atlas?"

I sat back. "I'm attracted to him. Relationships aren't pizza. There's no limit on the amount of slices before it runs out. I'm not gathering men like they're rings, one for each finger. It's not just me benefiting from the relationships either. Storm and Frost are getting closer. Dallas is like a brother to them. We're a family. Families don't have limits either. There's never a bad time to add more family members."

"Family." Jay mulled over the word. He glanced sideways at Atlas. "Is that how you feel? Like it's a family?"

"I guess so," Atlas said slowly. "If you think of Storm as the asshole brother who gives you shit for everything."

"What about Frost?" Jay's expression and tone were tight. "Is he a brother too?"

"I'm not leaving you for Frost either," Atlas told him. "You and I, we're... Us." His eyes were soft as he regarded the other player. "If you just want it to be you and I, I understand. But I'm attracted to Chelsea and Frost. I'd like to see where it goes."

Jay looked down at his half-empty bowl.

I held my breath. I wanted to get to know him better. I liked how protective he was of Atlas and vice versa. But if he wanted to walk away, I'd totally respect that. Life was too short to mess with something that wasn't broken.

"Jay." Atlas put a hand on his lower arm, between his wrist and his elbow. "I care about you a lot. Whatever you decide, we'll go along with it. Right, Doc?"

"Absolutely," I said. "We don't have to rush into anything. If Jay wants to think about it for a while, that's totally cool." He could take all the time he needed. I wouldn't push. Life was too short for that too.

"I never could say no to Atlas. I've seen the way he looks at you. And Frost too, I guess. He seems like a decent guy." Jay drew in a breath and blew it out slowly. "And I can't deny my own physical attraction to you." He nodded to me. "If Atlas wants to try, I'm in. With some conditions."

"Of course," I said. "Whatever you need." My heart raced. My clit throbbed at the prospect of being between them physically. Watching them touch each other. Being touched. Finding out what they were into and exploring their fantasies.

"I'm not moving in with Storm any time soon," Jay said. "If we ever do, it'll need to be a big place. I need my space."

"I agree," Atlas said. "Storm and I would literally kill each other."

I nodded. "We're already looking into somewhere bigger." I didn't elaborate. A cliffside mansion was a big step, and too soon to think about yet.

Not to mention the four of us might drive each other crazy in Storm's place and decide not to stay together. If that happened, I'd be devastated, but I'd be lying to myself if I didn't think it was possible.

"Anything else?" Atlas asked gently.

"You don't have a problem with me fucking Chelsea?" Jay asked.

Atlas looked from him to me and back again, his eyes darker. "Fuck no. If we're both in, then we're both all in. If that's what you want."

"You don't have a problem with me fucking Frost then?" Jay asked carefully.

Atlas looked surprised, but then swallowed visibly.

For a moment, I thought he might say he did, but then he said, "I don't. If that's what you both want. I... wouldn't mind watching."

Jay put his hand over Atlas' that still rested on his arm. "I can't imagine being with him without you present. Or with Chelsea. But I'm okay with you fucking either of them without me. You know how I am, sometimes I need my space. When I get overwhelmed, I have to take myself away."

He looked over to me, not quite meeting my eyes. "It's not personal. I just get...overloaded. If I don't have a quiet space, I feel like I'm losing my shit."

"That's completely understandable," I said gently. "The world is a lot. Families can be a lot. The good thing about families is that we take care of each other. And support each other. Anytime you need space, no one is going to judge you for taking it."

"Definitely," Atlas said. "And if you lose your shit, we're here for you."

"You always are," Jay said softly. He rubbed the heel of his hand up and down his forehead. "At our old club, some people didn't get it. They just want to be up in your space, you know? They think I'm aggressive or distant, or fucked up, or something. But I'm just in my own head, trying to deal with my shit."

"Did you ever—" This was a delicate topic to discuss, and he may not want to. If he didn't, I understood. I wouldn't push, but I was curious.

"Get a diagnosis?" he finished for me. "Yeah, I'm on the spectrum. Big surprise, right?" I wasn't judging him, but clearly people in the past had.

"I've seen you on the field," I said. "Your hyperfocus, it makes you one of the best players out there."

He blinked a couple of times, clearly surprised by my response. "Yeah, if I like something I fixate on it. I look at it in a different way from the other players. Like— Like analysing the best way to catch, and how other teams are playing so we can figure out where their weaknesses are."

"He's pretty amazing," Atlas said softly. "The sport needs more people like him."

Jay shifted uncomfortably. "Can we talk about something else?"

"Of course," I said. "Can I ask you both something?"

"Can we stop you?" Atlas teased. He had half an eye on Jay, until the other player started to relax. He was clearly in tune with Jay's moods and levels of overwhelm.

I liked him even more for it.

"You can try," I joked back. I sobered for a moment, "Obviously you like each other, but I'm wondering how far..."

"We've fucked," Atlas said. "Was that what you're asking? We don't make a big show of it, because other guys can be pricks. But we've more or less been a thing since we both started playing for the Devils—" He cut off his words, pressing his lips together.

Jay gave him the side eye. "What the fuck?"

Atlas rolled his lips and averted his gaze from Jay.

I frowned at both of them. "What is it?"

"You fucking didn't?" Jay gaped at Atlas.

Atlas glanced away for a while before looking back. "It wasn't going to let you come to Dusk Bay alone."

"You hated the idea of transferring," Jay argued.

"If I told you I did it for you," Atlas said, "you would have been pissed off. Plus we have to put up with Storm. That would piss anyone off. Some of my pissed-off-ness was genuine."

Jay shook his head. "You're out of your fucking mind."

"What was I going to do?" Atlas asked, spreading his hands to either side. "I wasn't staying at the Devils anyway. I might as well be here with you. I don't regret it. I get to be with you, and I met Chelsea. Between us, we can make the Smashers not suck so much."

"I think it's sweet," I said softly. "Following him here. You more than like each other."

That was becoming more and more obvious. Why else would Atlas have made that choice? It wasn't a thing someone did unless their feelings ran deep.

Jay looked uncomfortable again, but Atlas was visibly relieved.

"I love you," Atlas said matter-of-factly. He looked as though the weight of the world was literally off his shoulders. Like he didn't have to keep living up to his namesake.

I had the impression this was the first time he said those words out loud, but he'd wanted to for a long time.

"I love you too," Jay told him. "You're an idiot for transferring here, but I love you."

Atlas grinned and worked on finishing his dinner.

I smiled to myself. This was going to be interesting, to say the least. I knew both would get along well with Frost once they gave each other the chance. If Storm would let them.

As long as he was in control, he might let them do whatever they wanted to each other.

"So," Jay said after a few minutes of companionable silence. "Do you have... Permission to do what you want with whoever you want?" He raised an eyebrow at me.

"Do I need permission?" I asked lightly.

Atlas snorted. "Considering it's Storm Keller we're talking about, you probably need written permission, witnessed by thirteen other people, with strict stipulations of exactly what you can and can't do." He smirked and started to count the points off on his fingers.

"No screaming too loud. No having better orgasms than any he could give you. A limit on multiple orgasms. No—"

I laughed. "He's not that bad. He and the other guys understand that I can do whatever I want with either of you. They know all about you and I have their blessing. Believe it or not, I don't need their permission."

Yeah, Storm would say otherwise. He'd say he grudgingly gave his permission to me to enjoy them if I wanted to. If he did, I'd humour him. At the end of the day, as long as everyone was okay with it, I'd enjoy myself and these two guys, if that was what they wanted too.

Atlas and Jay both looked more than a little disbelieving.

I shook my head at them. "I promise you, there's no legal documentation with permission. Can you even imagine going to a lawyer with something like that?"

"Yes," Atlas said with a chuckle. "I'm pretty sure lawyers have seen worse."

"I wouldn't take that bet," I said. I finished the last of my dinner and rose to take the plates into the kitchen. "Does that mean you want to—"

"I do," Atlas said.

"Me too," Jay said. He looked tentatively eager. As though he wanted to, but he was taking a huge risk with himself, and maybe with his heart.

I blinked heavily, once, before looking directly at Jay. "Before we do anything, there's something you should know. Something about my past." Now had to be the right time, before we went any further. Whether Atlas liked it or not.

Before I could say another word, Jay knocked the breath out of me by saying, "You used to work at Flirts. Atlas told me on the way here. He thought if I found out suddenly, I might not react right."

It took me a solid minute to get my head around that and think clearly again. If Atlas told him on the way to my place, then he couldn't have told Bruce. In that case, who had?

Right now, that didn't matter so much as the fact it wasn't Jay. I wanted to hug him. I was so relieved. I didn't, not yet. We needed to finish this conversation first.

"There's no right or wrong way to react," I said evenly. "Whatever you did or said, I would have rolled with it." I was also relieved he already knew and wasn't running for the hills. Was that what he meant by not reacting right?

"I might have freaked out," Jay said ruefully. "Imagining you being in front of all those people, being vulnerable and touching them..." He shuddered. "I don't want to think about it. It's almost enough to give me a meltdown. The footy crowds are rowdy enough."

"So this isn't about you being upset about what I used to do," I said slowly. "It's the thought of you doing it yourself."

That made total sense. For someone on the spectrum who didn't like a lot of noise or physical contact, the thought would be daunting. The stuff of nightmares maybe.

"Exactly," he agreed. "I'm not going to judge you for doing it. Unless you're going to judge me for playing a sport where I get to tackle the shit out of people." His smile was tentative, but warm. Clearly dealing with people in general was a daily challenge. One he faced down like the badass he was.

I smiled back. "I would never judge you for playing rugby. Not when I love it almost as much as you do."

"Now that's out of the way..." Atlas said, not so subtly hinting at the fact we were still sitting at the table talking.

"Is it out of the way?" I directed the question at Jay. "You know about me and what I used to do and you still want to fuck me?" That was direct, but I knew he'd appreciate it. There was no point in trying to skirt around the topic. Especially with someone like him.

"I want to fuck you more than I did before," Jay

said. "You get me like Atlas does. Some people, they wouldn't have tried to tell me about their past. They would have let it creep up on me."

I did that with the other guys and the whole mafia shit, but not with this. Not when we were talking about intimacy. He should know what he was getting before he got me.

"I think we get each other," I said. "Let me show you."

Jay put his empty bowl beside mine and took one of my hands. Atlas took the other and between them, they walked me to my bedroom.

Chapter Seven

Chelsea

WE BARELY GOT THROUGH THE DOOR WHEN THE guys started taking my clothes off, layer by layer. They worked together to ease off my jumper and shirt, then shoes, jeans and socks.

"You were right," Jay said breathlessly. "She is gorgeous." He took a moment to admire me before tearing off his shoes and throwing them in the direction of the door like they offended him by being on his feet.

"She's more than gorgeous," Atlas matched his reverent tone. "She's incredible. Wait until you hear her come."

"I'm not sure I can wait," Jay said. He stepped around behind me and unhooked my bra before

Atlas tugged it down my arms and dropped it onto the floor with the rest of my clothes.

"You two are overdressed," I told them. I was standing in only my panties and they were still dressed.

"She has a point," Jay said. He hooked his fingers in the waistband of my panties and dragged them all the way down my legs. He waited until I stepped out of them before flicking them aside. He placed his hands on my ankles and ran them slowly back up my legs and over my ass.

"I don't know who has a harder ass, you or Atlas," he said. He straightened up to grab a handful of the other player's ass. He gave both a squeeze. "I think it's a tie."

"I think it's a tie between you and her too," Atlas said. "Let's call it a-three-way tie."

"It's about to be a three-way something," I said. Hell yeah, bring it on. "But you're still overdressed."

I turned to face them both and placed my hands on my hips. Eyebrows raised, I watched them, wanting, needing them both. Wanting and needing to see more of them.

They exchanged a glance before they turned to each other and started to help each other out of their clothes. Button down shirts, jeans and socks went flying. Everything until they were down to their boxer shorts. Both with erections on display under the silky fabric.

"That's better," I said approvingly. "I feel like I'm in a museum."

"Because Atlas is so old?" Jay teased. He grinned at his boyfriend.

I assumed at this point that was the right word for them. Even if they hadn't discussed it yet, it seemed appropriate.

"Fuck off," Atlas said with a laugh. "I'm only a couple of months older than you."

"Old enough," Jay said smartly.

"Have I told you recently you suck?" Atlas teased.

"Only if you're lucky." Jay turned to me. "I'm sorry, we're like this a lot." He actually blushed.

"I think it's adorable," I said. The more I saw of them, the more apparent their adoration became. I was starting to adore them both too. How could I not?

"Why does it feel like a museum?" Atlas asked, apparently done waiting to find out that 'vital' fact.

"Because you both look like statues," I said. I looked them up and down appreciatively. They were all muscle, carefully chiseled away by a master carver. With scars here and there for good measure.

"You're right, Atlas does," Jay agreed. "So do you. But I don't think anyone could imagine, or carve, bodies as beautiful as either of yours." His hungry gaze took us both in like we were dessert.

"Or yours," Atlas said softly. He grabbed the front of Jay's boxers and pulled him in for a heated kiss.

The moment their lips met, my blood ignited. Watching and listening to them, seeing the connection between them, the way their bodies responded to each other. Hot didn't come close to describing it. This was so much more than physical.

Expressing their feelings for each other like this, it was emotional too. Like somehow they'd held back before now, but they were done with that. They were going to embrace what they had, nurture it.

I wouldn't take any credit for it, but I'd support them fully. The same way I supported Storm and Frost's exploration of each other. The way I'd support any of them, in any way they needed.

They finally came up for air and both reached for me, grabbing my hands and tugging me towards the bed. We all fell in a heap of arms and legs and skin. Laughing, the guys slipped out of their boxer shorts, letting their erections spring free, finally giving me a good look at their cocks.

Atlas' was slightly longer, but Jay's was thicker. Neither were pierced, but they were both as much works of art as the rest of their bodies were. Thick, engorged and already leaking pre-cum.

Jay lay on one side of me, his mouth descending on my breast, drawing my nipple between his lips and sucking softly.

Atlas lay on the other, lightly kissing my mouth before sliding his tongue between my lips and tasting my teeth and tongue.

I kissed him back, letting our tongues tangle, tasting the risotto he'd eaten for dinner. That and a hint of salt, maybe a little of the flavour from Jay's mouth. Either way, it was delicious and I wanted more.

Jay moved over to the other nipple, giving it the same careful treatment he'd given the first. Swirling his tongue around my sensitive peak, sending heat right between my legs.

I was already wet, but they were quickly making me drenched.

Jay moved away from my breasts, slowly kissing down my body. Down between my legs where he parted my thighs and tasted my pussy with the tip of his tongue.

I quivered. It wasn't going to take much for me to come.

"Yum," Jay said. He smiled up at me before diving back in for more.

Atlas went on kissing my mouth, while rolling my nipple between his thumb and forefinger. Pinching lightly, then firmer when I moaned my appreciation.

"You like it a little rough?" he asked.

"Yeah, I do," I whispered. "I like it every way you can give it to me."

"Every way, hmmm?" he asked. "That leaves a lot of possibilities."

I looked over at him, wondering what he was thinking. I got the impression he could be creative.

"It does, doesn't it?" I said.

"Jay," he said.

Jay stopped mid-lick to look up at us. At some signal I couldn't see, he moved out from between my legs. Both of them pulled me off the bed and moved me over to stand in front of my tall dressing mirror.

Jay dropped himself to his knees in front of me, before opening my legs again and pressing his face back between them.

Atlas stood behind me, looking over my shoulder. "Isn't that a pretty sight?" He cupped my breasts and palmed my nipples while Jay feasted on my pussy.

I looked down at him, but Atlas caught my chin with his finger and tilted it back up.

"Keep your eyes on the mirror. Watch yourself while he tastes you. Watch my hands on you."

I watched my reflection as both men lavished attention on my body. I watched my hips roll as Jay brought me closer and closer to coming.

Atlas dragged a hand down my back to grip my ass. He pressed his fingers between my cheeks and over my rear hole. "Look how I'm touching you." He wiggled the tip of his finger into my ass, pushing it in deeper. "You like that."

"Yes, I do," I said. "So much."

"Good," he whispered. "You're going to come. You're going to watch yourself come. Say it back to me."

"I'm going to watch myself come," I said. My cheeks were pink, my whole body on fire from their touch. I'd had lots of sex, but never watched myself like this. It was erotic and beautiful at the same time.

"Make her come," Atlas said to Jay. "I want you to hear her."

Jay looked up at him and nodded slightly, without breaking the rhythm of his teasing licks.

My eyes fluttered closed.

"Open your eyes," Atlas ordered, in a tone that would have made Storm proud. "Watch yourself come."

I forced my eyes open just as the orgasm took hold of my body. I watched myself rock back and forth against Jay's face. His head bobbed, drawing out my orgasm for longer and longer. Making the bliss last for a minute, two. Maybe too many for me to count.

As I came, Atlas impaled me further and further on his finger. So deep that by the time I came down, he was all the way inside me. I had no words for how good it felt.

Finally, he pulled his finger free and bent me forward until the palms of my hands were pressed against the glass of the mirror.

"Now you're going to watch me fuck you," he said softly. His reflection was beside mine as he stroked his cock a couple of times. Finally, he positioned himself outside my pussy and pressed himself inside me. With one stroke, he was all the way inside.

I gasped aloud at the sudden sensation of being

completely filled. So perfectly full, all the way to the brim.

Over my shoulder, he watched himself pull out of me before slamming back in again. Over and over he thrust, harder and harder. He gave me everything, holding back nothing.

Jay was still on his knees, watching us, his hand curled around his own cock. He stroked himself in time with Atlas' thrusts, his hips rolling along with mine.

"You feel incredible," Atlas whispered near my ear. "I knew you would. Your pussy was made for me. For us."

At a nod from Atlas, Jay rose on his knees and started to stroke my clit with the tip of two fingers.

"We want you to come again," Jay said. The first thing he'd said in a while. He continued to pump himself with one hand while he worked me with the other.

"I want you both to come," I whispered.

"Atlas," Jay said. "I want to see you come inside her."

"Fuck, Jay," Atlas whispered in protest. "You're going to make me come, just saying that."

"Good," Jay said unapologetically. "Come inside her. Fill her up. Just like you've filled me up before."

He worked me harder, his fingers grazing Atlas' cock at the same time as he teased my clit.

"Mmm, please," I begged. "Come inside me."

Atlas grunted and let go, slamming into me a couple more times before he came hard, crying out and spilling himself inside my body.

At the same time, I came again, harder and faster than before. My cries matched Atlas', like a beautiful choir.

I was just coming down when Jay got to his feet, pumping himself again until he came, squirting cum over my stomach and hip. Leaving me warm and sticky.

"Fuck, that was hot," Atlas said. slowly and carefully, he pulled out of me and helped me to straighten back up.

"It is for starters," Jay said. His hand on my upper arm, he guided me back to the side of the bed. He sat me down and knelt between my legs. "It's only fair to clean you up."

Once again, he parted my legs and started to lick Atlas' cum as it leaked out of my pussy.

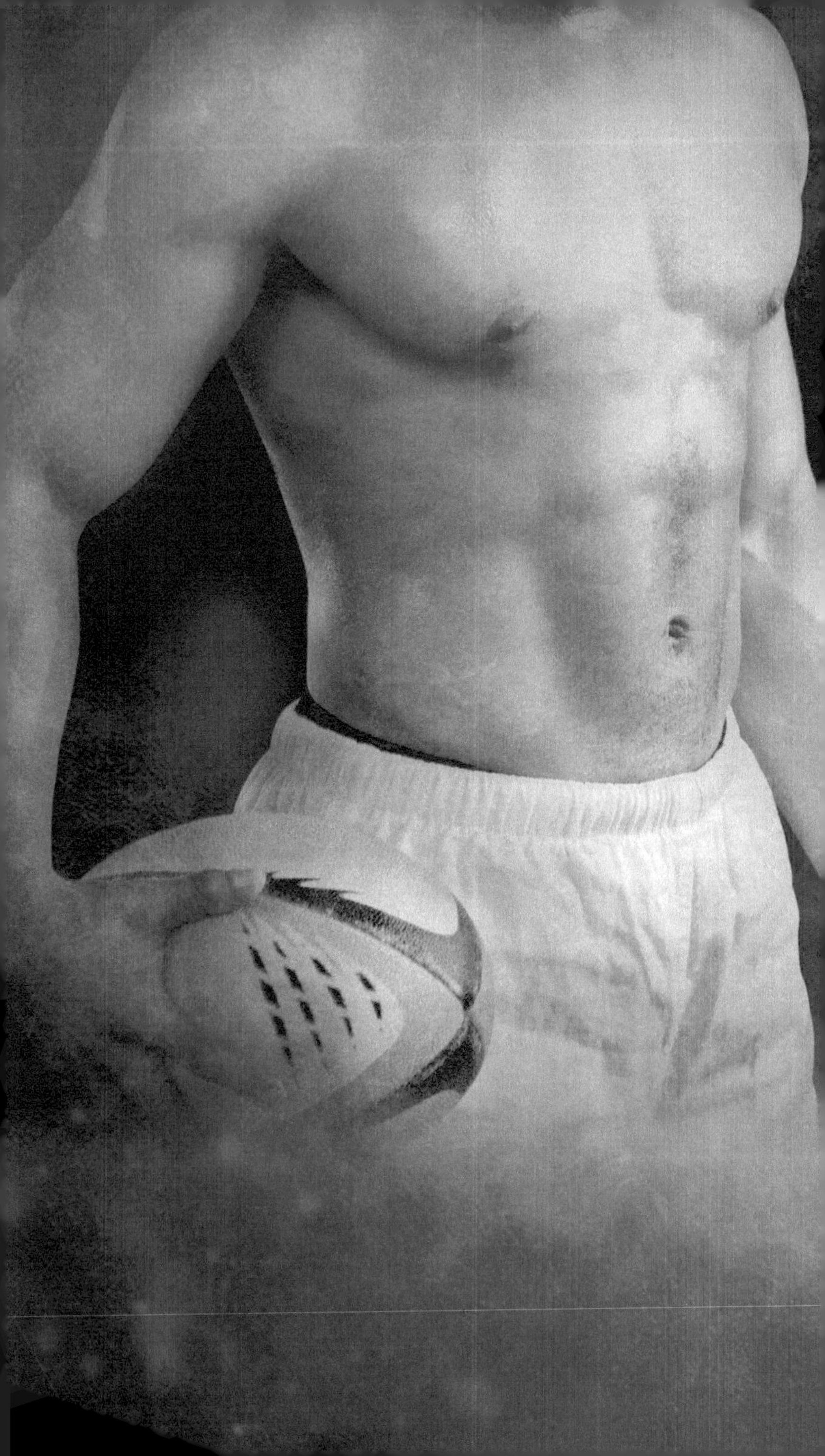

Chapter Eight

Chelsea

"I'M STARTING TO THINK I SHOULD HAVE borrowed some goalie padding from the Dusk Bay Demons," I whispered to Frost. "Then it might be safe to stand between them."

Storm and Atlas stood on opposite sides of the visitors' locker room. Every so often, they eyed each other.

So far, no one took a swing.

"I know what you mean," Frost whispered back. "The whole flight over, I was expecting one of them to say *something* to the other. Then it would have been on. I think Dallas wanted to shove them out the door somewhere over the Pacific."

"I've tried to get them to talk to each other, but it's worse than herding cats." I sighed.

"Who's herding cats?" Cautiously, Jay stepped over to us, socks and footy boots in one hand.

"We are," Frost said. "I'm thinking we need to put both of them in a room and not let them out until they talk to each other. What do you think?"

"I think we might open the door to two dead bodies," Jay said regretfully. He glanced over to Atlas, then to Storm, irritation etched on his face.

"That would take care of the problem of them arguing with each other," Frost said slowly. "But I don't like the end result too much. Let's put that in the maybe pile."

Obviously, he had no intention of actually doing that.

At least, I thought it was obvious. Jay looked like he wasn't quite so sure. Or maybe he wouldn't have minded if Storm was gone.

"What's going in the maybe pile?" Dallas joined us in the corner of the locker room.

"Letting Atlas and Storm fight their differences out," Frost said. "If they were hockey players, they'd spend all their time in the penalty box after punching the shit out of each other on the ice. Can't really get away with that on the footy field."

"Not when they play for the same team," Dallas

agreed. "I assume they've already compared cock size?"

"I'd say they've had a look," Frost agreed. He glanced at me and raised his eyebrows.

"About the same," I said. Both were big and knew how to use them. They wouldn't sort out anything that way.

"They're about as fast as each other, so a foot race wouldn't prove anything," Frost said. "Can Atlas sing?"

Jay grunt-laughed. "If you think cats having their tails pulled sounds good, then yes. Otherwise, no."

"They could have a competition to see who's the worst singer," Frost said. "Storm is pretty bad too. On the other hand, we'd be torturing ourselves."

"I think that can go in the maybe pile too," I said. I liked my eardrums undamaged. Not to mention, they couldn't help it if they weren't good at singing; we didn't need to make a point of proving it.

"Can they cook?" Dallas asked. "We could see who does that better, and get a feed at the same time."

"I don't think they're ready to share a kitchen," I said regretfully. That was a good idea, but not if Atlas was inclined to slip poison into people's food or drink. He might decide it was a good opportunity to get rid of Storm.

"They'd be even in an arm wrestle," Frost mused. "What about a poetry slam?"

I bit back a giggle. "I'd love to see that." I cleared my throat and affected my best poet's tone.

"There was once a woman from Dusk Bay.
She went out for a walk one day.
Saw a bunch of footy players naked.
Then didn't know what to say."

I grimaced. "That was terrible."

All three guys smiled. The cleft in Jay's chin became more pronounced. He really was pretty adorable.

"It wasn't that bad," Jay said. "You should have ended with, *they weren't as hot as Jay.*"

I clicked my fingers and pointed at him. "I knew it was missing something. It's much better that way."

Coach Stanley called for them to get out on the field to warm up.

Jay made a face, but sat down to pull on his socks and boots.

I noticed he was always the first one to take them off and the last to put them on. He must not like the way they felt on his feet, so he waited until the last possible minute.

He clearly found ways to adapt, so he could fit into this world of professional football.

I had to admit, that was hot. He wasn't going to let anything stand in the way of what he wanted, not even himself.

"Do I get a kiss for luck?" Frost asked. "First game of the season." He looked excited and ready to get out there and play.

I leaned over and kissed his cheek. As a doctor, I was allowed in the locker room, but I didn't want to push it too far.

"Me too," Dallas said. For once, he seemed focused on the game ahead and not on fucking me. For that, I was grateful. He could easily let me be the distraction he didn't need.

If that happened, I wasn't sure how we'd deal with it. I didn't think he did either, so he forced himself to get his head in the game, where it belonged.

I kissed his cheek, then carefully offered one to Jay once he stood. He let me kiss him, but quickly moved to the door and out onto the field.

I understood, he was never going to be inclined to public displays of affection. Or private ones unless he was totally comfortable with a person. Not everyone was cuddly.

They all filed out, leaving me to follow Doctor Stuart, to stand beside him on the sidelines.

The crowd in Auckland was loud tonight, excited for the game. The stadium was packed and the night was clear if not warm. In a handful of weeks, it would be cold out, but for now it was pleasant. The perfect night for a game of football.

"This is my favourite part," Doctor Stuart said. "Getting to watch a game up close."

A shiver of excitement passed through me. "I've been looking forward to this. And hoping like hell they don't need us." I wouldn't be a very good doctor if I *wanted* them to get hurt.

"That's always the hope," he agreed. "You know who to keep an eye on, to make sure they don't exacerbate any past injuries."

I held up my board with my notes on it. "Yes I do. Including Atlas' nose." A broken nose wouldn't stop him from playing, but if anything connected with it, it would hurt like a bitch. A fact, no doubt, he was well aware of, and trying his best to avoid.

"Wouldn't want to do further damage to his good looks," Doctor Stuart said with a hint of sarcasm.

If he was anyone else, I might have thought he was trying to insult Atlas, but it was just his dry humour. He was definitely not trying to get a rise out of me.

What would he think if he knew what Atlas did to Bruce? I had a feeling he'd have no choice but to contact the police. Given my brother already conducted the autopsy on the dead GM, Doctor Stuart would have no proof to offer them. He might end up looking like he was out of his mind.

Still, he'd do what he was obligated to do.

So would Atlas. Bruce might not be the only one the team lost.

No, we'd all be better off if Doctor Stuart never knew the truth. I liked working with him and I had a lot to learn. I much preferred it if no one murdered him.

I realised I hadn't responded to him. "Definitely not. We wouldn't want to ruin any of the guys' good looks. Just think what that would do to all those endorsements."

"They might get more of them," Doctor Stuart joked. "Don't women love a damaged hero?"

"I suppose we do," I agreed. I loved them in my romance novels, and judging by the guys I was involved with, apparently I loved them in person too. As long as they were only damaged, not broken.

The crowd roared as the home team trotted out onto the field and started to warm up.

Some of those boys were huge. Taller and broader than ours. Each one looked more fierce than the last.

They warmed up quickly before forming a line to do the Haka, the ancient Maori war dance, designed to intimidate the enemy. The shouts, growls and stamping would have intimidated the hell out of me if I was their enemy too.

In this context, it was always entertaining. I could watch them perform all day. There was something hot about the performance. Something incredibly masculine and powerful.

The crowd cheered as the players finished and moved into place.

A light breeze picked up, ruffling my hair and clothes.

Everything about this moment was perfect. I was finally *here*, right where I was supposed to be. Watching my guys and the rest of the team taking on the tough New Zealand team. I could almost not get my head around it.

Me, Doctor Chelsea Miller, was *here*, in New Zealand, in a professional capacity. An actual member of the team, not just a hopeful anymore.

"It never gets old," Doctor Stuart said. "Any of this. If it ever does, then you need to find another job."

"I can't imagine ever getting bored of this," I said with a contented sigh.

"I never will," Doctor Otis Skinner stepped over to join us. He'd been deep in conversation with the opposition's team doctor.

I'd caught the words 'water' and 'promising' as he spoke, as animated as I'd seen him in our brief interactions together. He was generally composed, always calm and in control. This was a man who wouldn't take a swing at anyone. The sort of man you didn't turn your back on, if you knew what was good for you.

Where other people were closed books, Otis Skinner was one with the shrink wrap still in place.

"Settling in well?" Doctor Stuart asked him.

"Well enough," Skinner said. His dark eyes regarded me before turning back to Doctor Stuart. "This team is an interesting one."

"That it is," Doctor Stuart said lightly. "A mix of skills and abilities. I'm sure we have a lot to learn from each other."

Skinner looked at him like he didn't think he'd

have much to learn from Doctor Stuart, but he nodded once, slowly. "I'm sure."

"Doctor Stuart was saying you have an interest in aqua therapy," I said.

"That's correct," Skinner said simply.

"I look forward to finding out more from you," I said. I felt as though I was babbling to fill the awkward silence.

"Good," was Skinner's response. Once again, his expression revealed nothing but a hint of annoyance. Was that aimed at me, or something else? I couldn't tell.

My lips moved, but no more words came out. What could I say to that anyway?

Hopefully, he wouldn't prove difficult to work with, but if he was, I'd roll with it.

Whatever his problem was, I wouldn't make it mine.

I made a quick mental note to insist my guys not kill him if he was cold to me, or to them. At this rate, I'd need to make a list for them. And for my brother. He'd probably enjoy having Skinner down in his workroom, chained to the ceiling. If only to see what it would take to get a response from him.

I sighed softly and turned to the field as the game began.

Chapter Nine

Dallas

There was barely time to pat each other on the back following our win, before we were herded onto a plane back to Australia.

Chelsea sat with Doctor Stuart and Otis Skinner, leaving me to sit in the rear of the plane with the other players. Storm and Frost sat together. Atlas sat behind them with a barefoot Jay, and I sat across the aisle next to Ferris Ramsey.

"Good game." I fastened my seatbelt and adjusted the strap.

"Yep," he said.

He was a man of few words, but he was an excellent hooker. The rugby position, not the other kind, as far as I knew.

"We should have won by more than two points," I added.

"We would have if the referee was paying attention," Storm growled. "He totally missed that knock-on by Franklin."

"We still would have won," Frost pointed out.

Storm's jaw worked back and forth. "They wouldn't have got that last try if the ref pulled them up."

"Yeah, but they did," Atlas said, pressing his face in the gap between the sets in front of him.

Storm swivelled around. "Don't try to bullshit me and say you're okay with it. We both saw. I know you were pissed off too."

"Didn't say I wasn't." Atlas leaned back. "It was a bad call."

"Did you two just agree on something?" Frost asked.

"Nope." Storm crossed his arms over his chest and looked straight ahead.

"Yeah, you did," I said. "We all agree it was a bad call, right Goat?" I turned back to Ramsey, who was looking out the window.

"Right," he said simply.

I nodded and swivelled back to the others, point proven. Or not disproven.

"I agree too," Jay said. "Frosty is right, we would have won anyway, but we deserved to win by more."

"Fucking right we did," Atlas said. "If you ask me, Franklin is a prick. He shouldn't have got away with it."

Storm turned around and looked through the gap. "That's what I was going to say. Next time we play them, one of us needs to stay on his ass and keep him in line. Seems like his team isn't doing it."

Frost leaned forward and grinned over at me. I nodded in return.

It seemed like the two of them found common ground; hating on the referee and Franklin Hicks. I also shared their dislike of the big fullback. His arrogance would make the combined egos on this flight look humble. He thought he was God's gift to rugby, but I wanted to smash my fist into his face every time I saw him.

Since he thrived on attention, I ignored him instead.

"Works for me," Atlas said. "Asshole needs his ass kicked. Instead, he gets all the big endorsements. Anyone would think he's good-looking, the way they carry on about him."

"I mean, he's not ugly," Frost said with a shrug.

Storm and Atlas both stared at him like he was out of his mind.

Frost shrugged. "I'm just saying is all. It's not like I have plans to go there. He's not my type anyway."

"I'm pretty sure his type is inflatable," Storm said dryly. He was about to add something else, but closed his mouth.

It didn't take a genius to figure out what he was going to say. At this point in a conversation, he would have suggested Franklin paid for sex. He wouldn't disrespect Chelsea by making a comment like that now.

"Makes no sense," Ramsey said. He turned from the window and stared at Storm.

"What makes no sense?" I asked.

His brow creased deeper. "Inflatable woman. Prick like him would pop her."

His tone was so deadpan, it took me a moment to realise he'd made a joke. When it sank in, I burst out laughing.

The other guys followed a heartbeat later.

"Goat has a good point," Storm said. "A prick like him would pop her like a balloon." He grinned at Ramsey, like he just realised the guy existed.

Ramsey nodded and returned his attention to the window as the plane lifted off from the tarmac.

"I never knew you were funny," I told him.

He shrugged. "Sometimes."

I suspected it was more than sometimes, but he kept his observations to himself.

"I went to school with a guy who thought he was hilarious," I said slowly. "He kept cracking jokes and doing stupid stuff. Slapstick things, you know? The only person who thought he was funny was him. It's better to tell one joke that's actually funny than a million that aren't."

Ramsey turned back to me slowly. "What happened?"

"To that guy?" I asked. "I think he went into accounting or something like that. Shame when you think about it. He liked trying to make people laugh. If he had better jokes, he could have been a stand-up comedian." I shrugged. "I guess you can't always follow your dreams."

Ramsey grunted. "Can if you want to."

"Are you following yours?" I asked. This was the first time we had anything in the way of a conversation. For some reason, I felt compelled to keep it going.

His dark blue eyes suggested he wasn't inclined to respond, but finally he said, "Mostly."

"Not completely?" I asked.

"Wanted to be a fullback," he said. He pressed his lips together hard, a visible sign of his lingering bitterness.

"Oh." I nodded slowly. "That must have been frustrating." I'd always wanted to be a second rower. That was where my talents lay, just like his lay in being a hooker. I saw lots of guys frustrated at not being able to play the position they wanted. Coach put us where we could be the most effective, regardless of what we thought about our own skills. In the end, it was only the team that mattered.

Ramsey shrugged. "Better than not playing."

"Yeah," I agreed. "It's definitely better than not playing. What would you be doing if you weren't?"

"Not fucking inflatable women," he said with a smirk.

I snorted a laugh. "Me neither bro, me neither." Why would I need an inflatable woman when I had Chelsea? "You should hang out with us sometime." We'd never really done that since we started playing together, apart from the occasional drink after a game.

He looked at me, then over to the other guys. "You have room?"

"For one more? Yeah, we do. Stormy will be

happy to know his inflatable woman is safe from us." I grinned.

If the fullback had a problem with Ramsey spending time with us, he'd have to get over it. Realistically, I suspected he might object to Ramsey less than he objected to Atlas. If he didn't, that was too fucking bad. In spite of what he thought, I didn't need his permission for anything.

"I heard that, fuckwit," Storm growled. "I don't have an inflatable woman either. If I did, Atlas would be jealous."

Atlas barked a laugh. "Piss off, Keller. As if I'd be jealous of you."

Storm turned around. "Not of me, dickhead. Of the inflatable woman because I'd be fucking her and not you."

"You're not my type," Atlas told him.

"Back at you," Storm said. He turned back around, effectively ending the conversation for now.

"Just when I thought they were getting along," I said quietly.

"Alpha males," Ramsey said.

"Maybe we should call them 'Goat,'" I said. "They act like a pair of goats trying to head-butt each other."

"Both like Doctor Chelsea," Ramsey observed.

"We all like her," I said.

I was head over heels in love with her, but he probably saw that on my face. I didn't try to hide it, and I got the impression he saw everything, always watching, observing. Missing nothing, stashing away his thoughts for later.

In the past, guys like him made me anxious. They always had the best blackmail material, because they saw things no one else paid attention to. Had I done anything for him to hold against me? Probably, but nothing came to mind right now.

"Tricky," he said.

"It can be," I agreed. "Most of us get along pretty well, otherwise it would be a pain in the ass. We'd spend half our lives fighting over her."

"You don't?" he asked.

"Only Storm and Atlas, but we're hoping they'll get over themselves sooner or later." I glared over at both of them, but they were deep in conversation with Frost and Jay.

"I should steal her," Ramsey said.

I whipped my head back toward him. "What the hell?"

He smiled, the soul of innocence. "Might help them see what they have."

"I didn't realise you had a devious side either," I

said. "You think if she's interested in you, they'll stop fighting with each other and work harder to keep her?"

He shrugged one shoulder. "Can't hurt. She's cute."

It shouldn't surprise me he'd noticed that about her. I saw him looking, but from a distance. Like he was curious, but didn't dare to approach.

That was understandable, given she was usually surrounded by a few of us. Getting her alone for long enough to have a conversation with her, would have been difficult. Especially given he wasn't much of a conversationalist. That is to say, I didn't think he was. I should have tried harder, but I was trying now. I could see us being friends, if he was down for that.

"She's adorable," I agreed. "You might be onto something here. We could try to make them jealous and see if it brings them together."

"Better chance than we'd have with an inflatable woman." He smiled.

I laughed. "I think we can all agree not to bring any inflatable women into this situation. Not unless it would help in some way."

"How?" he asked.

It was my turn to shrug. "I don't know. I wouldn't rule out anything, to be honest. If they keep barking at each other the way they have, they're going to drive us all up the fucking wall."

"Yep," he said. "I told them."

"I noticed," I said.

Since right around the time I met Chelsea, he was telling Storm to back off and stop being a prick to Atlas.

Atlas and Jay both had a difficult time settling into the team and Storm's animosity hadn't made the transition any easier. Fitting into a new team was hard enough without that kind of bullshit.

Although, it was nothing new when it came to rugby teams. When you formed a tight bond with a group of guys, it was difficult to let anyone new in. Especially when they didn't seem to *want* in.

I admit, I hadn't tried very hard with either of them myself. Apart from adding to the chorus— telling Storm and even Frost to back off—I hadn't made an effort to be friendly with the new guys. Granted, I didn't do friendly very well, but I could have tried.

"They need to listen better," Ramsey said.

"Now who's the alpha male?" I teased.

He puffed out his chest a little. "Always me. Biggest cock too."

My gaze dropped to his groin and back up again.

"In your dreams," I said. "Mine is the biggest." I'd seen all of the others, and mine definitely held its own.

"Who's dreaming?" he asked. "I know the truth."

There was a hint of mischief in his blue eyes. One I'd never seen before, or at least never noticed. Of all the things I would have expected of him, funny as hell wasn't one of them. I appreciated his subtle brand of humour. It was better than someone who tried too hard.

I laughed and shoved my shoulder into his bicep. "I think I underestimated you. Your ego is a match for anyone here. Maybe you should have been a stand-up comedian."

"I am the GOAT," he said smugly.

"The greatest of all time," I said with a laugh. "We should have given more thought to that nickname."

"It fits." He nodded. "I'm the GOAT who rams. Watch your woman. I might steal her for real."

"I won't let you steal her," I said. "But I might let you share."

Chapter Ten

Chelsea

"MR KING WILL SEE YOU NOW." BRUCE FERGUS' personal assistant must have kept her job, because she was still behind the same desk. She looked more anxious than the last time I saw her, but a new boss would have that effect on most people. Including me.

"Thank you," I said. I smoothed down the sides of my skirt and stepped into the new GM's office.

Dominic King sat behind his desk, eyes on his laptop. He wore a dark suit, and a dark tie that contrasted with his crisp white shirt. His hair was smoothed back off his forehead, black except for a hint of grey at his temples.

I waited for a moment, but he didn't look up.

"You wanted to see me?" I asked finally.

He seemed to be speaking to all of the staff, one by one. Presumably, this was my turn.

Finally, he looked up, dark brown eyes regarding me, long and slow. By the time he nodded, I felt like he'd stripped off every layer of my clothes, leaving me standing bare in front of him.

He glanced back at his laptop. "Doctor Chelsea Miller. Youngest member of the medical team. Just out of university." He could have been reading off his screen, but I got the impression he wasn't. That he knew who I was.

"That's right," I said. "I'm excited to be a part of the team."

"Close the door," he said.

That wasn't exactly the response I was expecting, but I took a couple of steps back and pushed it until it clicked shut.

Hoping like hell he didn't mean for me to be on the *other* side of it.

"I know the team will benefit from your appointment," I said smoothly.

"Of course," he said. He closed his laptop and rested his clasped hands on top of the lid. What was it with the men from the Sydney Devils? First Otis Skinner, now Dominic King. They were both aloof and had an air of smug-as-fuck around them.

"What can you bring to the team?"

Was this another job interview? My pulse immediately raced, nervous he was about to fire me. He owed me no loyalty. He was here to run the team. If he decided I wasn't the best choice, then he'd be within his rights to toss me out.

"Enthusiasm and loyalty," I said, chin raised with confidence. "Up-to-date knowledge and a good work ethic. I've already proven I can work well with Doctor Stuart."

I hadn't had a chance to prove I could work with Skinner yet. Hopefully that wouldn't be held against me. Especially since it wasn't something I could help.

"Do you believe any of that is more important than experience?" he asked. His gaze remained firmly on my face, but I still felt naked in front of him.

"Actually, I do," I said. "I've worked with doctors who have been in the profession for so long they don't accept new practices. They believe because they've done something a certain way for so long, it must be the only way. I think flexibility is important for the team. The ability to adjust to a quickly changing scenario. Just because a method is new, doesn't mean it isn't valid and valuable."

"You find flexibility important," he stated. He

seemed to be trying to get at something. I couldn't quite work out what.

"It's very important," I said. "In all aspects of life, we have to be able to adapt to change. If we're not flexible, we get stale." Not to mention flexibility was fun in the bedroom.

"All aspects," he echoed.

Once again, I got the impression he was trying to get at something.

"Excuse me, Mr King—"

"Dominic," he corrected softly.

"Dominic." I took a breath and started again. "Are you thinking of putting me in a different position?"

Whatever he was thinking, I didn't believe he was about to fire me. If he was going to, he would have done that already, not waste his time with this conversation. He didn't seem like the kind of man who wasted time.

One of his eyebrows quirked upwards a fraction. If I wasn't watching, I would have missed it. My racing heart ratcheted up harder.

He knew. I didn't know how he knew, but he did. He'd been alluding to it from the moment I walked through the door.

"I—" I didn't know what to say. I couldn't just blurt it out, in case I was wrong, but I knew I wasn't wrong. He knew it too. I saw that in his dark eyes. Right now, he was holding all the cards. The entire pack.

"Did you think I wouldn't look into everyone here?" he asked softly. "This is Dusk Bay. No one should take a...position here without thorough research." His choice of words was deliberate.

I swallowed hard. "I'm not ashamed."

Now, I was almost certain I was wrong after all. He *was* about to fire me. Okay, that would suck, but I wasn't going to let him make me feel bad about what I did in the past. How I made a living.

"Why would you be?" His brow wrinkled. "Every player who steps out on the field uses their body. It's their profession. Using it one way is not so different to using it another. To suggest otherwise would be hypocritical. Wouldn't you agree?"

"Definitely," I said, not bothering to hide my surprise. "I hadn't thought about it that way, but I agree with you. Both are...a form of entertainment."

"Both of which I enjoy." He steepled his fingers. "I'm sure you appreciate it's best not to advertise this to the rest of the world. Exotic dancing isn't what one might consider family friendly."

"Depends on the family," I said without thinking.

That earned me a faint smile. "I suppose that's

true. Generally speaking, it would be best to keep this quiet."

"I've been trying to do that," I said. "I don't want to make trouble for the team. If it got out, the press would have a field day."

I didn't want to think about that shit storm. I'd have to hide in Storm's apartment until the worst of it blew over. How long would it take? That was anyone's guess. Sometimes the press cycle moved on quickly, sometimes it didn't.

Did he know the truth of what happened to Belinda Simmons? I decided he probably didn't. If he did, I wasn't entirely sure he'd object.

People like him, and people like me, we did what we had to in order to protect the things we cared about. It wasn't a big stretch to picture him pulling a gun on her, or someone like her. It wouldn't even surprise me if he had Reuben Brantley on speed dial. Or the other way around. I wasn't aware of every person who worked for the Brantley family. He could easily be one of them.

"That they would," he agreed. "You understand if that was to happen, I'd be forced to fire you. For the good of the team, not because I believe it's the right thing to do."

He seemed irritated by the idea that anyone

would force his hand. In that, he reminded me of Storm. My way or the highway. Or to put it in Dusk Bay terms, my way or a shallow grave.

"Does that mean you're not going to fire me?" I asked.

Was that too brazen? I decided it wasn't. I'd given him my honesty, and all I asked in return was for him to be honest about this. If he was about to let me go, he should get it over with.

He pressed his fingers against his lips for a moment before lowering them and responding. "I happen to agree with what you said. Experience is a good thing, but not when it's overshadowed by a lack of flexibility." He smiled slightly again. "Skinner can be inflexible in his own way, and so can Doctor Stuart. I trust you'll be able to bring a sense of flexibility to the team that will keep things fresh."

"I'll certainly try," I said. I didn't think either man was going to listen to many of my suggestions, but I wouldn't let that deter me. I'd work to the best of my abilities and make suggestions when they seemed appropriate.

"I'm sure you will," he said. "From what Doctor Stuart has told me, you're ambitious. I wouldn't expect anything less from anyone who grew up in the city. I imagine you develop survival instincts from an early age."

Once again, I could see he was well informed. Was that why he'd been chosen to be the new GM? Had his appointment gone through the Brantley family? Nothing much would surprise me at this point, least of all that.

"You could say that," I agreed. "You also learn the value of loyalty. If you give it to the right people, you get it in return."

His eyebrow twitched again. "Is that your way of suggesting I should be loyal to you, because you're loyal to me?" His face was a mask, hinting at an amusement, but mostly hiding what he thought about that suggestion.

I added him to the list of people I should never play poker with.

"It wasn't my intention, but I don't see why that shouldn't be the case," I said. "Like I said, I work hard. Everything I do, I put all of myself into it. I'm sure you'll see that."

"My loyalty is to the Smashers," he said slowly. "That includes everyone who works for the team. Which is exactly why I intend to keep your secret."

The words "for now" hung in the air between us. I hated the idea he had this over me, but the only other option was to walk away, and I wasn't doing that.

"I appreciate that," I said honestly. "Like I said, I'm not ashamed, but I realise the bomb that could go off in my face if this got out."

"We don't want...bombs to go off in your face," he said, his words carefully chosen.

"We don't want bombs to go off in anyone's face," I said. Or any other weapon, for that matter.

"Agreed," he said smoothly. "We'll all do our best to prevent that from happening to anyone here. Which brings me to one final matter. Your relationship with several of the players."

He had me worried for the second time in a handful of minutes.

His lack of concern about my dancing was one thing. Fraternising with the players was another. It might be the one thing he'd be forced to fire me for.

Or he might insist I stop seeing them, in which case we were going to have a problem. If he did, he might quickly end up like Bruce had. That would be a shame.

"Yes?" I asked carefully. "Is it a problem?"

"At this point in time, no," he said. "If it becomes a problem, then we'll address it. What players and staff do on their own time, is their own business, unless it has an impact on the team. Then it becomes my business. Understood?"

"Crystal clear," I said. "We're all very much aware of the importance of me not distracting them from their job. And vice versa. In public, we're professional."

In private, we were anything but.

"Good. Make sure it stays that way. I believe you'll be an asset to the team, but that's up to you. If you're willing to give us everything you have, then you'll do well. If not—"

I had the feeling he wanted to say, "If you're willing to give *me* everything you have, you'll do well."

"The team is everything to me," I said. "I intend to keep giving it everything."

Chapter Eleven

Chelsea

I REACHED THE BOTTOM OF THE STAIRS LEADING into Ice's workroom. The air inside was cold. Cold enough to make me shiver. I wrapped my arms around myself and tried not to look at the person that hung from the chains today.

"Who's Dominic King?" I asked.

Ice turned to me and smiled warmly. "Chels, I wasn't expecting to see you today." Hands covered in blood, he stepped over to kiss my cheek.

"In answer to your question, he's a problem." He stepped over to the sink and start to wash his hands, seemingly oblivious to the groans of his victim. "Mannix thinks he sees himself as a rival to the Brantley family."

I sighed. "Of course he does. Working for him is going to be a problem, isn't it?"

Wasn't that just life? As soon as I get my dream job, I might be forced to walk away from it after all.

"Not necessarily," Ice said. He grabbed a towel and started carefully drying his fingers, one by one. "You might be able to get information from him using more subtle methods than me."

I rubbed my temples with my thumb and the tips of my fingers. "Did any of you encourage Atlas to kill Bruce Fergus? Because all of this is too convenient. You know I want to stay out of all of the mobster shit."

"I know, but all that mobster shit still wants you." He grinned. "You'd be surprised how liberating it is when you embrace it, instead of trying to push it away. Take our friend here." He gestured towards the bloodied victim. "We're having a lot of fun together."

"It doesn't look like they're having fun," I remarked.

Ice clicked his tongue. "Of course he is. He's learning all about the limits of what he can tolerate."

"What use is learning something like that when he'll be dead soon?" I asked.

Ice tossed the towel aside and adjusted his bun.

"He'll die understanding himself better. How could he not be grateful for that?"

"I have no idea," I said dryly. "So, about Dominic King. And Bruce Fergus."

"I didn't say anything to Atlas about killing anyone," Ice said. "But I can't rule out someone else telling him to. Mannix might have. He doesn't tell me everything. Almost everything, but not *literally* everything. If he didn't, why would Atlas do that?"

I quickly explained his reasoning.

Ice nodded slowly. "Remind me later to tell him he did a good job. If I knew Bruce was going to hire someone else, I would have dealt with him myself. Just think, he could have been chained up beside our friend here." He cocked his head and smiled, pleased at the idea.

"He didn't deserve to die just because he wasn't going to hire me," I said.

"Of course not," Ice said reasonably. "But if he refused to listen to reason, and it sounded like that was the case, then of course we'd do that for you. That's what we do when we love someone."

"Other people give boxes of chocolates," I said dryly.

"Some of us do both." He gestured toward

himself. "Or we bring you pyjamas and socks. Do you need more?"

"No." I held up a hand. "I'm good on socks and pyjamas. Thank you. What is Dominic King doing to make you think he's going to cause trouble?"

"I could ask you the same thing," he said. "You're here talking to me about it. What did he do, and do I need to clear my schedule this afternoon to make time for him in here?"

"Not this second," I said. "He knows about me working at Flirts. He says he'll keep quiet about it." Reluctantly I added, "For now."

"Ah. Classic subtle blackmail." Ice nodded. "I'm going to go out on a limb here and suggest he knows we're related."

"You think he wants to use me to get to you?" I asked. "Or to manipulate you in some way?"

Ice looked thoughtful, lips pursed. "It's what I'd do if I was him. I'd find out exactly who was working for me that I could use to benefit myself. It's exactly what any member of the Brantley family would do. Except maybe Zeke."

"And now they're going to use me to benefit them," I said, the last couple of words ending with a sigh.

"Your boyfriends too," he agreed. "Especially

them. Their connection to us is newer. It's possible Mr King doesn't know about it yet. It would be a good idea if he didn't find out."

"He's not going to find out from me." I wrapped my arms around myself again. "How long before the Smashers are hunting for a new GM?"

"That depends on Mr King," Ice said. "And what our orders from the boss are. He'll be watching closely, waiting to see if Dominic King makes any moves. And Otis Skinner as well. From what I've heard, those two are thick as thieves."

"Should I worry about Atlas and Jay? They used to play for the Devils. Is it likely to be a coincidence all four of them are here now?"

"Probably not," Ice said. He picked up a knife and started to clean the blade. "That's a conversation you might have with them. Subtly, of course. If you find out they're up to something, let me know and I'll deal with them."

Now I pictured the two guys hanging from the ceiling, their wrists in chains, bodies covered with random incisions. Or not so random, given my brother would be the one doing the incising. He never did anything without a reason.

"Daze trusts them," I said.

"Daze is a good judge of character," he said. "You

may not have anything to worry about, but I don't believe in coincidences. There's probably more to what's going on than either of us know."

"Are you trying to tell me you don't know everything?" I teased, wanting to lighten the mood. Given the still-groaning man on the other side of the room, that wasn't an easy feat. Not for my mood anyway. My brother was as unshakable as always.

Ice chuckled. "I know, it's shocking isn't it? Big brothers are supposed to know everything." He put down the now-clean knife and stepped over to offer me a hug.

"In this case, I *should* know everything. One of my missions in life is to keep you safe and happy. It's harder to do that when not every player is showing their cards."

"How powerful is Dominic King?" I rested my head on his shoulder and absorbed his warmth. He always made me feel safe, even if I wasn't.

"He has growing connections," Ice said. He ran a hand up and down my back, slowly, soothingly. "And, from what I gather, growing ambitions. So far, he's managed to keep his nose relatively clean. If he's going to try to take a shot at Reuben, it won't be soon. He'll take his time and build his empire, if he can."

"Starting with the Smashers," I said.

"No offence, but I think it has more to do with Dusk Bay than it does with the team," he said. "An opportunity arose and he took it."

"Because Atlas created the opportunity." I kept turning that detail over and over in my mind.

My brother was right, it was too much of a coincidence to be an opportunity Dominic King happened upon. If Atlas hadn't killed Bruce, he couldn't have been appointed GM.

Was I just a convenient excuse? A cover for what Atlas did? Did he care about me at all? Did Jay?

"Would you prefer I talk to Atlas?" Ice asked. "I have a way of getting people to...open up." He grinned at his own joke.

"I'll talk to him first," I said quickly. "People have a way of not lasting long once you get your hands on them."

If there was a chance Atlas wasn't working for Dominic King, then he didn't deserve to end up here. Not to mention it would piss Reuben off if we killed someone we shouldn't. If he ever found out about it, that was. My brother had a way of covering his tracks, even from those he worked for.

"By the time they get in here, they weren't going to last anyway," Ice said. "Take this guy here." He stepped away from me and jerked his thumb towards his hanging victim.

"What did he do?" I should know better than to ask, but curiosity let the words slip from my mouth.

"His stepdaughter," Ice said. "She was underage. And not consenting."

His eyes flashed with anger, all directed at the man in chains. My brother was nothing if not protective of other people. Women in particular. If anyone fucked with them, he was only too happy to fuck back, twice as hard. And several times as bloody.

I made a face. "Okay, I guess I can agree he deserves to be here." Anyone who would do that to a child should be chained up and tortured.

"I agree." Ice smiled. "That's why he currently has no balls and no penis. Those were the first things to go when he got down here. He watched while I incinerated them in my oven over there. He didn't seem to enjoy the smell of cooking meat."

My brother could have been talking about what a nice day it was outside and how cute puppies were. His words chilled me right to the bone.

I hadn't looked that closely, but I glanced down now and winced. That was the source of much of the blood on him and on the floor at his feet.

The man groaned, the sound of despair echoing

through the space. Pure agony and grief for his lost body parts. Hoping like hell he'd be dead soon and the suffering ended.

"Satisfying, isn't it?" Ice asked. "Now that you know what he did."

"That's not the word I'd use," I said. "You could have ended him quickly."

Either way, he'd end up dead. A slash across the throat, or a bullet in his brain would have stopped him from reoffending. I hoped like hell the step-daughter was okay. It was likely she'd never know what my brother did to dispense justice for her.

I hoped she never did. It sounded like she'd been through enough without knowing this room existed, much less what took place in here. It would give a sane person nightmares.

"It's not as much fun if he doesn't suffer for what he did." Ice picked up a clean knife and looked at his victim appraisingly, trying to figure out where to slice next.

"I'll have to take your word for it," I said.

"Why take my word for it when you can find out for yourself?" He offered me the knife, hilt end first.

I held up my hand to decline the offer. "I wouldn't want to deprive you of your fun."

I knew full well he saw it as exactly that, as well

as his own brand of justice. He got off on what he did. Unlike other people, he'd at least admit he was slightly unhinged. He never bothered to hide the fact. Not when it came to his job.

"I don't mind sharing," he said lightly. "Especially with my baby sister. You might find you actually enjoy this."

"That's exactly what worries me," I said. "That I'll like it. I think I'll leave you to it. I need to go and talk to Atlas."

I hoped like hell I could get to the bottom of what he did, especially if I could do it without him realising. If he was working on the opposite side, then he could very easily lash out at me for digging into him.

Just when I thought life couldn't get more complicated, it turned ass-up.

Chapter Twelve

Dallas

"What's wrong?" I nibbled on Chelsea's earlobe while she looked out the window toward the ocean. "You've been lost in thought since you got back. Do I have to hurt anyone?" Because I totally would. Hurt, not kill. Unless I had to.

She leaned back against me, letting me put my arms around her. "I'm not sure. I mean, no you don't have to hurt anyone. I just mean, I'm not sure if anything is wrong. It might, and then it might not."

"I'm going to need you to elaborate," I said. "You have something on your mind. You know we're here to listen any time you want to talk." I hated the idea she might have a problem she didn't feel comfortable talking to one of us about. What were families for if they weren't for sharing problems?

"I know, I just..." She exhaled softly.

"Whatever it is, chances are we're already involved," I said. "You're not trying to spare our feelings, are you? I mean, Storm doesn't even have any."

Storm, who was in the kitchen with Frost, cooking dinner, called out, "I heard that. Yes I fucking do."

"Of course you do." Frost patted his bicep. Those two were getting more joined at the hip by the day.

I laughed softly, letting Chelsea feel my body rumble, even if the other two couldn't hear me. It was too easy to get a rise out of the big fullback.

"I'm not trying to spare your feelings," Chelsea said. "It isn't about that."

"What is it about then?" I pressed. "Because something is clearly bothering you. Are you not getting enough orgasms?"

She laughed. "That is definitely *not* a problem I have."

"Are you sure?" I ran my hand over her flat stomach and down to the apex of her thighs. "Because I love nothing more than giving them to you."

Like she always did, she melted in my arms. I made a note to insist she tell me what was on her mind later. For now, there was only one thing on mine.

That was leaning her forward until she pressed her palms against the window and undoing the front of her jeans. I pulled them down her legs and her panties with them.

While she stepped out of them, I worked the buttons of her shirt loose and pulled it down of her shoulders. I unhooked her bra, and that went next, dropping to the floor.

If anyone looked up, or from across the road in Luchesi Tower, they'd see her in all her naked glory.

They'd see me kneel down behind her and spread her legs before sliding a couple of fingers deep into her. She was already nice and wet. I licked her ass cheek before biting down hard enough to make her squeal.

Smiling to myself, I bit her other cheek, then brushed my tongue over the bite, to soothe the pain. I wanted to leave my mark on her, but I wanted to take care of her too.

She wiggled her ass in my face, making me smile. She was so fucking sassy. Just for that, I bit her again. Her firm, round cheek was delicious.

I worked my fingers in and out of her, making her wetter. Enjoying the feeling of her tight muscles around my calloused fingers. If I could, I'd crawl up inside her and live there. Inside her soft, wet heat. I'd spend my days rubbing her G spot and making her come, over and over again.

For now, all I did was work her with my hand. Drive her to the edge of coming before slowing down, then driving her hard again.

I took her to the brink of coming once more, before sliding my fingers out and waiting until her breathing slowed.

She groaned in frustration. "Dallas..."

"Chels," I said in the same tone of voice, teasing her.

She let out a choked laugh. "You suck."

I chuckled. "When you put it that way." I stripped out of my pants and pulled her down to the floor with me, her legs straddling me, her pussy right above my face. Her mouth was right above my cock.

I gripped her hips and pulled her down so I could run my tongue up and down her wet seam. Her pussy was even more delicious than her ass.

She groaned and wrapped her mouth around my cock, sucking while grinding against my face.

It was my turn to moan. The woman's mouth was as perfect as her pussy. No one sucked me the way she did. No one ever would. She was it for me.

She was mine and I was hers. There would never be anyone else. Not for me.

I held her above me, devouring her like she was my last meal. If I died with her riding my face, I'd die happy.

She moaned, long and low before coming hard on my mouth. Her whole body went still. She took her mouth off my cock and cried out as her release spilled from her pussy, over my chin and down my cheeks.

It was so fucking hot, I came the moment she latched her lips back around my cock. I couldn't help myself. My balls tightened and I exploded right into her mouth.

We both sagged, panting for a few moments before she turned her face and swallowed down my cum.

"Good girl," I said breathlessly. She was better than good. She was fucking amazing. "I love you."

She looked back at me for a moment and said, "I love you too."

That was the first time she said those words to me. They stole what breath was left in my body. Hearing them was better than having her come all over my face.

"I got you a little wet." She swung her leg off me

and crawled over to lightly touch my face with the tips of her fingers. "I've never done that before."

I probably didn't need an ego boost, but hearing her say I made her squirt for the first time was better than seventeen Christmases all at once.

This woman.

I smiled. "First of many." Now I knew what it took, I'd do everything I could to make her do it again. And again. And again. And...

"That was fucking hot," Frost said.

I didn't know when he'd stepped over to sit on the side of the couch, but he was sitting there now, watching us. His track pants were down to his thighs, his cock was wrapped around his hand.

Chelsea clicked her tongue. "It would be a shame to make you do that yourself."

"It would." Storm stood to the side of the room, his arms crossed over his chest. "Crawl to him and suck him off."

A smile on the corners of her lips, she dropped to all fours and slowly crawled across the hardwood floor to Frost. She placed her hands on his thighs and lowered her mouth, making his cock disappear past her lips.

Frost's eyes rolled back in pleasure. "So... Fucking... Good..." Her head bobbed as she sucked, his hand tangled in her hair. "Chelsea... Fuck... I love you."

She tilted her head to look back at him. She slid her mouth off him long enough to say, "I love you too," before bending back down and continuing to suck.

His eyes widened slightly in surprise, but he smiled. Content to know she felt the same way he did.

He bucked his hips, moving in time to her sucking, his eyes half closed. Lost in a world of bliss. "I'm going to come," he whispered.

A moment later, he did, grinding against her lips and losing his load in her mouth. He grunted a couple of times, thrust a few more. Fucking her mouth for all he was worth.

Finally, he sagged back against the couch, blinking to clear his head.

She slipped her mouth off him and rose to step over to Storm. She kissed his mouth, long and slow, before squirting Frost's cum into his mouth.

His eyes widened in surprise, but he leaned back and swallowed down the mouthful.

"Now that was hot," I whispered. I had no interest in tasting their release, but watching them share it was something else.

A moment later, Storm had his pants down to his knees, and Chelsea bent over the back of the couch. He grabbed her hips and positioned his cock before slamming all the way into her.

They both let out a cry, then he pounded into her. His teeth were pressed together, his jaw tight, all of his effort and concentration focused on thrusting into her as hard as he could.

"Fuck...yeah. So fucking incredible. So fucking *mine*." His teeth were gritted as he spoke from behind them. "You always take everything I give you. You take it so fucking well."

She was. Watching him fuck her pussy her was mesmerising. The slap of skin on skin, the sheen of sweat on both of them. Everything about this was erotic as hell. She was pure, tantalising sex, in the body of a beautiful, intelligent woman. Seeing a man as powerful as Storm claiming her, owning her, was seared into my brain like a hot brand.

Who needed a video when I could memorise the moment and relive it whenever I wanted?

Sitting back and observing was almost as good as taking part. Knowing she was getting what she needed, that was everything. She deserved to be fucked like a queen. Over and over until she couldn't walk anymore. If she wasn't satisfied, then we weren't doing our jobs. We weren't worshipping her enough.

"Harder," she groaned.

Her hair got loose from her ponytail and now hung around her face, damp with sweat. Right on her ass, beside one of Storm's hands, was a bite mark from *my* teeth, red and angry. My mark on her, next to his fingers.

He liked to leave bruises, and judging by his grip, he was going to. If anyone was in any doubt she was owned, they only had to look at her ass. The signs were right there, perfectly eloquent.

I didn't think he could fuck her harder, but he did, driving in over and over again, until the legs of the couch scraped forward from the force.

"I'm going to come!" Chelsea shouted. Half the tower would have heard her if the place wasn't soundproofed.

I half-wished they could. The whole world should know she was being fucked. They'd be envious of us if they did. Jealous we had her and they didn't.

"Not until I tell you," Storm warned.

She moaned. "I can't—" She was all but sobbing now, in frustration.

"Yes, you can," he insisted. "Don't you dare

fucking come until I say so." He slowed his thrusts, sliding in and out of her with even strokes. Making the most of every single moment. Enjoying being buried deep inside her. Wanting to make the moment last, but clearly struggling to keep from pitching himself over the edge into blissful oblivion.

She dropped her head. Her breath was a couple of harsh, frustrated pants. She must have been right on the edge, forcing herself to stay there and not pitch over.

"Storm," she begged in a whisper. "Please..."

"Okay, you can come," he told her.

A moment later, they both came, groaning and grunting together, her crying out while he filled her body with his release.

He sagged over her, gathering her up in his arms. "Good girl. I fucking love you, woman." His voice was a whispered growl, barely loud enough for us to hear.

She leaned back against him and closed her eyes. "I fucking love you too."

I didn't know what changed to make her say it back to all of us tonight, but after she got cleaned up, we were going to talk. Even if I had to tie her down to get her to open up, I *would* do that. Then I'd fuck her again.

Chapter Thirteen

Chelsea

"Out with it." Storm crossed his arms over his chest and looked down at me, his best firm expression on his face.

"Out with what?" I said lightly. I sat cross-legged on the couch, wearing one of the guys' track pants and another one's T-shirt. Both were too big, but they were so comfortable, I couldn't bring myself to regret rummaging through drawers to find them.

"Whatever is bothering you," Frost said more gently.

Dallas sat beside me and snorted. The good cop, bad cop routine wasn't lost on him either, it seemed.

"You went to see someone, and came back looking more upset than you were when you left,"

Storm said. "Where did you go? What the fuck has you looking like you need to watch your back?"

I closed my eyes and exhaled softly out my nose. Was it that obvious? Apparently it was. I hadn't been trying to hide my thoughts, not really, but it seemed I should have.

"Is it a journalist?" Frost asked. "Is someone poking around again?"

"It's possible," I said. I leaned my head against the back of the couch. "I spoke to Dominic King. He knows about my past."

Storm dropped his hands to his side. "Fuck. Is he going to—"

I held up my hand. "I don't think so."

I told them about the conversation. Everything except the veiled threat, that King would expose my past if it suited his purposes to do so.

"That wasn't who you went to see this afternoon," Frost observed.

"I went to see my brother." I looked down at my lap. "He has a theory that Atlas killed Bruce Fergus for Dominic King. So the GM position would open for him." I let them absorb my words.

"Why?" Dallas placed one of his hands on my knee.

I explained what my brother said about Dominic King wanting to accumulate power in Dusk Bay.

"He thinks Atlas is working for King?" Storm asked. He looked ready to chew rocks. His jaw worked in obvious annoyance.

"He doesn't know," I said. "If he did, then him killing Bruce had nothing to do with me after all. Isaac thinks I should talk to Atlas. Try to find out what his agenda is." If he had one. This was nothing more than speculation. Again. Fuck knows we were wrong the first time. We could be wrong this time. I wanted to be. I hated doubting any of them, not when Atlas and I were becoming close.

"I knew that guy was a prick," Storm snarled. "He's working for the fucking enemy."

"Maybe," I said. This was exactly why I was reluctant to say anything to these three. Storm, in particular, was always going to jump to conclusions. His dislike for Atlas wouldn't let him respond any other way. "It's only a theory. Everything could have gone down the way Atlas said it did. And for the reasons he said they did."

"I know you want to think the best of him," Frost said slowly.

"So do you," I pointed out. "It's just... It's one hell

of a coincidence that he made exactly the opening Dominic King needed."

"Fuck coincidences," Storm said. "I don't believe in them. I knew there was a reason I didn't trust Atlas fucking Underwood. Or Jay fucking Lang."

"Yeah, it's because you only trust Storm fucking Keller," Dallas said darkly. "You've never given Atlas a chance. Now you're ready to throw him under the first bus, based on a guess."

He looked at me and his expression softened. "I know it's *your* guess, but it's still just a guess. Do you think he'd work for the people who want to rival Daze and the people she works for?"

"I don't want to believe it," I said. "I think he's a good guy. There's always the possibility he doesn't know who he's really working for."

That happened before. Probably often. Someone gets hired to do a job and the person doing the hiring lies about who they are. Mob folk weren't always known for their honesty. Not when it suited them to twist the truth.

"But you do," Storm said. "Otherwise you would have talked to him already. You would have let him rule it out." He cocked his head at me, challenging me to disagree with him. The problem was I couldn't, not exactly. But it wasn't that simple either. I needed to make them understand that.

"There's one thing I learned growing up here in Dusk Bay," I said slowly. "It's to be very careful who you accuse of...anything. We already know Atlas is capable of killing. I'm scared I might back him into a corner and—"

"Then you don't go anywhere near him," Storm interrupted. "If the motherfucker lays a hand on you, I'll rip it the fuck off his wrist and smack the shit out of him with it."

"I hate to say it," Dallas said, "I agree with Storm. Unless we know we can trust Atlas or Jay, then you shouldn't be around them."

"I agree with both of them," Frost said. "I like Atlas, but if there's any doubt in your mind about him, I'm not willing to take the risk with you."

I wanted to argue, but this was exactly the kind of shit I'd spent my whole life trying to avoid. "Then I don't go alone," I said. I closed my eyes again.

"What is it?" Dallas asked.

"My brother suggested his boss might want me to spy on Dominic King," I said slowly. I didn't need to open my eyes to know what their reaction would be. "If he asks me to do that, he won't be giving me a choice."

Now I opened my eyes. "He might want you to do the same thing."

"I can do that," Frost said a little too quickly and with a bit too much enthusiasm.

"So can I," Dallas said. "We'll be around him anyway. Enough that no one will suspect us, or think we're paying too much attention to him. We know how to play it cool."

Storm grunted. "Better be worthwhile. I'm a fucking footy player, not James Bond."

"You'd make a perfect James Bond," Frost told him. "You look good in a suit."

"You all do," I said. How had I gone from dating three hot football players, to dating three potential mafia spies? Did they really understand what they were putting their hands up for? If anyone so much as suspected what they were suggesting, they could end up dead. Or with 'accidental' injuries that would end their careers.

In the back of my head, I felt like I was dating five. I hoped like hell Atlas had a good excuse for what he did. I didn't want to think he'd looked me in the eyes and lied to me. If he did, his life would be significantly shortened by my brother or one of the three guys I was currently sitting with.

"You'd look amazing in a slinky black dress,"

Dallas said. "The kind with a slit all the way up your leg." He squeezed my thigh.

"And just enough fabric to cover a hidden knife," Frost said. "But to show lots of cleavage. Not too much, just enough to distract the enemy."

"I think you've been watching too many movies," I said flatly.

They both smiled. They didn't seem to mind the teasing accusation. Neither denied it.

"It would be a scalpel," Storm said. "Because she's a doctor."

"Yeah, we figured that was why," Frost said. "That would be easier to explain than a knife. You never know when you might need to perform emergency surgery."

I shook my head at them, but they'd effectively lightened the mood.

"Nothing says 'subtle' like a slinky dress. People are less likely to pay attention to me if I'm wearing—" I waved down at my present outfit.

"Not a chance," Dallas said. "It doesn't matter what you wear, people will pay attention. You could wear a paper bag and people would stare."

"They probably would stare if I wore a paper bag," I agreed. "I'd look pretty strange."

"You'd look adorable," Frost said. "I might get myself one, so we can match."

Storm shook his head. "You guys are ridiculous. Let's focus on what's important here. We need to deal with Atlas."

His words brought the mood back down to Earth with a crash. He was right, but the return to reality wasn't all that welcome. Joking around was much more fun. Something I'd like to do a lot more of, but apparently that would have to wait until later.

"We need to *talk* to Atlas," I corrected. "No killing him." I looked around at all three of them, but my firmest expression was for Storm. We didn't need him to run off half cocked and punch Atlas' lights out based on what was nothing more than a theory. We could be wrong.

"I agree not to kill him if he's not fucking with us," Storm said. "If he is, then all bets are off."

His grey eyes looked like a thundercloud about to burst. He was so certain he'd been right about Atlas all along. What if he was? What if he wasn't? Would he let up on the other player if he found out we were all on the same side? What would it take for them to trust each other? Was it too much of a stretch to hope they might like each other some day?

A girl could hope. Judging by the wrinkle on Frost's brow as he frowned, he was hoping the same thing. On the other hand, he'd be almost as willing to kill Atlas as he would to fuck him. I knew which one I'd prefer to watch.

Spoiler alert: fucking.

"We should do this away from the stadium," I said. "Away from Dominic King. If he has any idea we're having this conversation, he might come after us regardless of Atlas."

"Another candidate for having his hand ripped off and getting smacked with it," Storm said. He mimed pulling off his left hand and hitting someone with it repeatedly.

"That's very specific," Frost said. "Do you have some fetish about ripping off hands? Or just smacking?" He grinned.

Storm snorted. "Both. Only when people deserve it." He eyed me sideways. "I'll also smack Chelsea if she decides to try to talk to him without us. Or does anything to risk herself."

"Don't threaten me with a good time," I said lightly. "Or better yet, do. I like a good time." I could still feel the pinch of Dallas's teeth on my ass cheek. The sting of the marks he left behind. Right beside the bruises from Storm's fingers.

"I'm seriously thinking of handcuffing you to my bed and leaving you there," Storm said. "You'd be safe from all sorts of shit like that."

"As much as I like that idea, when you guys play away, there'd be no one to feed me," I said.

Not to mention other things I couldn't do for myself if I was tied to the bed. I didn't mind feeling helpless in the right context, but that wouldn't be it. Especially if, in spite of Storm's assurance, someone broke into the apartment. I'd have no way to run or even fight back. No, better to use the handcuffs when the guys were around. Anything else would be potentially dangerous. And not at all fun.

"I could stay," Dallas said. "We could alternate between feeding and fucking. With the occasional bath in between."

"Now *you're* threatening me with a good time," I told him.

That sounded pretty fucking perfect right now. But I couldn't lie back and do nothing until I knew what Atlas's deal was. And Jay's. And, given his growing closeness to both of them, Ramsey. Dallas told me about the conversation they had on the plane and that he seemed like a good guy, but he could be in it up to his eyeballs as well.

"I'd never threaten you," Dallas said. "But I'm

always ready to give you a good time." His hand wandered up my leg and under the waistband of my track pants.

Chapter Fourteen

Chelsea

"Coach said you wanted to see me." Atlas stepped through the doorway into the infirmary. His tone was light, but his expression was one of concern.

"I thought I should check up on your nose," I said as easily as I could.

My mind raced, palms sweating. I bet anything my brother wouldn't be so anxious under the same circumstances. Hell, Sadie would be cooler than I was.

I'd have to give her a call later to get together with her. We hadn't had much time to talk about me moving out, except for her being happy for me. She already had one of the girls from Flirts moving into my old room. Hopefully they'd get along as well as Sadie and I had.

Atlas shrugged. "It's fine. Is that all there is, or did you want to see me for...something else?" He wiggled his eyebrows and stepped closer to me.

Doctor Stuart was off today and Skinner was down in the pool working with some of the injured players. We had the place to ourselves, which was why I asked him to come here now.

I took a step back and cursed myself for doing it. So much for not being suspicious. If he didn't suspect anything from that, he would a moment later when Storm, Frost and Dallas stepped out of the meeting room.

"What is this?" Atlas asked. He eyed them warily. His whole body stiffened when Dallas stepped around to stand guard in the doorway.

"Why are you here?" Storm demanded.

"Chelsea asked me to come," Atlas replied. "Why are *you* here?" He was looking as pissed off as a cornered lion, ready to strike back if necessary, when the moment presented itself.

"I don't mean here in the infirmary." Storm rolled his eyes as though the question was obvious. "I mean here at the Smashers."

"What do you think I'm here for, dickhead?" Atlas snarled. "Same as you, I'm here to play footy."

"Is that all?" Frost asked. Once again playing good cop to Storm's bad cop.

Atlas didn't meet his eyes. "I don't know what you're getting at."

"Bullshit," Storm snapped. He lowered his voice. "We know what you did to Bruce. Why?"

"Because he didn't want Chelsea working here," Atlas said, looking at him side on. "Are you trying to tell me you object to her being here? Because that would be a load of shit. You want her here as much as I do."

"Was that the only reason?" Frost asked. "Because of Chelsea?"

Atlas stared at him like he was out of his mind. And yet, there was still something in his expression and body language that said to me there was more to it than he claimed.

"What else might there be?" he said evasively.

Storm crossed his arms and glared at Atlas. "How about the incredible coincidence that a manager at your former club was appointed GM right after Bruce died?"

"I don't get to choose the general manager," Atlas

pointed out. "They must have thought he was the best person for the job. Which he is. We won the premiership last season, remember?" As if anyone could forget. "The Sydney Devils rugby club is full of talent."

"Like Otis Skinner," I said softly.

Atlas twitched. "Yeah, like him." He seemed as fond of Skinner as he was of Storm.

"What's going on?" Jay stopped in the doorway and peered past Dallas' shoulder.

Atlas turned his head slightly towards him. "They seem to think there's more to what happened to Bruce than I've told them."

"Right." Jay all but pushed Dallas out of the way and closed the door, shutting us all in. "Are you going to tell them the truth?"

"Don't say we can't handle it," Storm said.

Atlas rubbed his forehead with the heel of his hand. "I'm sure you can. You might not want to."

"You can't tell us that and not tell us everything," Frost said. He looked antsy as hell, itching to find out what was going on.

"Fuck," Atlas said under his breath. "But not here. I don't want to risk being recorded." He lowered his hand. "Telling you could get you all killed. If there's any chance we're overheard, you don't want to suffer the repercussions. Trust me."

"As far as I can spit you," Storm muttered. "If you walk out of here right now, what guarantee do we have that you won't run? Or go off and tell your boss we're onto you?"

"We work for the same people," Atlas said, becoming visibly exasperated.

"Says you." Storm didn't look so certain.

"Says me too," Jay said. "Atlas is right. We shouldn't talk about this here. We've probably said too much already." He shot Atlas a worried glance.

"Name the place," Storm said. "Not your place."

"Yours, if you can guarantee we won't be overheard," Atlas said. "You're not going to trust any other location I name."

"Nope," Storm agreed. "After training. My car."

"I'll drive myself," Atlas said. He lifted his chin, not giving a centimetre. His brown-gold eyes were as steely as Storm's grey ones, hard and determined.

"I don't—" Storm started.

"I'll drive with you," Jay said with a frustrated exhale. "If it'll make you feel better." He looked like a lamb who just offered to be placed on a spit and rotated over a fire for several hours.

Storm looked reluctant, but nodded. "Fine. If either of you try to screw us over..."

"Same to you," Atlas told him. "You haven't given me reason to trust you either."

"We're all going out on a limb," Dallas said. "If we're going to make this work, then we need to." He looked over to me.

"Dallas is right." I wanted answers as much as the rest of them, but I needed to trust all of them. I wanted to, I really did. I cared about everyone in this room right now, even when they were at each other's throats.

"Finish training, then we meet in the car park," Storm said. He nodded like the matter was settled.

"I still need to look at Atlas' nose," I said. "To make sure it's healing well."

Storm, Frost and Dallas all looked at me and Atlas. Clearly uncertain as to whether they could leave me alone with him.

I had to make a decision, right now. Did I trust Atlas, or didn't I?

"I'll be fine," I said finally. "It'll only take a moment." I stepped over to open the door. Gave them all a meaningful look, which they responded to with reluctance.

Jay was the first to step towards the door, followed by Dallas, then Frost.

"You too," I said to Storm, who looked as though he had no intention of going anywhere.

"I don't care if he stays." Atlas gave him a long look before stepping into the treatment room. Something of a warning to keep his distance, and not try anything in the absence of the other guys. They reminded me of a pair of dogs circling around a bone, or the carcass of some other animal. Each wanting to take a bite, but being held back by the presence of the other.

"Then I will," Storm said. He waved to the others out the door before leaning against the door frame and watching.

"He's a stubborn prick," Atlas remarked.

"I'd say you have that in common," I told him.

He grinned. "Guilty. But only on that count."

I looked searchingly into his brown-gold eyes.

He lowered his voice. "I promise, I'll tell you everything. Just not—" He stopped the moment Otis Skinner walked through the doorway into the infirmary. The other doctor gave Storm a glance, but walked past him, into his own office.

"Not here?" I finished for him. What did Skinner's presence have to do with anything? There was clearly something to it. Something more than them knowing each other from the Sydney Devils. Atlas was wary of Skinner. Was vice versa also the case?

Right then, I had more questions than answers. Including, what would my brother do? Knowing him, he'd have all the answers by now. By torture, or some other method. Either way, people opened up to him. I didn't have his charm, not that I knew of. If I did, I didn't know how to use it quite as well.

"Definitely not here," he agreed. "Be careful what you do here. And who you do it with."

"I never liked cryptic clues." I stood in front of him and ran the tips of my fingers up and down his nose.

He stood still, eyes focused on the side of my head. "I never liked giving them. But I like you alive. And I like myself alive. I am also aware the team's performance is better with Storm around. For now. He's a reasonably good fullback."

"Did you just admit you like him?" I teased.

Atlas' gaze swivelled towards the door and he smirked. "Nope. I appreciate his skills as a footballer, not as a... I'd say human being, but I'm not sure if that definition fits." He smirked at the other player.

"Fuck off, Underwood," Storm said. "I'm as human as you are. More so."

"Are you always going to try to push each other's buttons?" I asked with a sigh.

"I'm not trying to push anything," Storm argued. "Just stating a fact. And defending myself after he tried to attack my humanity."

I raised an eyebrow at Atlas.

"He's fun to toy with," Atlas said. "Every time I throw out the bait, he takes it. I guess his mother didn't teach him to ignore guys like me."

He looked amused as hell. Having four older sisters, he must have learnt young to have a thicker skin when being teased. Between that and being in the public eye, he had to let it roll off his back like it was nothing. I suspected it got to him more than he let on. He wasn't like Storm who wore his heart on his sleeve. And his attitude.

"My father told me to use my fists with guys like you," Storm said. "If they give you shit, you give them bruises. Or broken bones." His sidelong glance at Atlas suggested he'd happily give him both. Not in the same way he liked to leave bruises on me. They were a handful of words from coming to blows, and now was not the time for that. Not in the infirmary and not with everything else that was going on.

"It's time to put that behind you," I said. "You

can't go around punching people just because you disagree with them."

"I don't," Storm said. "I use my verbal fists. If I used my real ones, Atlas would look like dog food." He seemed impressed at his own restraint. Me, I was just glad he held back and hoped like hell he continued to.

"You're all class, Keller," Atlas told him.

"Fucking right I am," Storm agreed. "The classiest." He stood up a little straighter, even though he clearly understood Atlas was trying to push his buttons yet again.

Atlas waited until I lowered my hands from his nose and leaned down to brush his lips over mine. "The only classy person I see around here is Chelsea."

He leaned down further to whisper in my ear. "I promise, you can trust me. I'll tell you everything. Just to do me a favour and stay safe until then." He straightened up and his gaze flicked toward Skinner's office again.

A shiver travelled up and down my spine. Skinner was a closed book, but was he a threat? Atlas certainly seemed to think so. His explanation couldn't come soon enough.

"I'll be okay," I said lightly.

Maybe Frost was right and I should start carrying around a scalpel strapped to my thigh. Or maybe I was paranoid.

The question was, would that get better or worse, depending on what Atlas had to say?

It was going to be a long afternoon, waiting to hear what that was.

Chapter Fifteen

Chelsea

"I trust you can attend a training session without supervision." Skinner appeared from his office the moment Atlas stepped out the door. "I have two more patients to see this afternoon." He looked weary, like he didn't want to bother with me.

I managed to keep myself from bristling in irritation. I'd completed my exams and passed everything. Graduation was just a formality at this point. As was receiving my degree to frame and hang on my wall.

"I can deal with whatever arises," I said with a confident nod.

"Arrogance won't get you far here," he remarked.

I blinked at him a couple of times. "Excuse me?" *Now* I was bristling. I forced myself to be calm, reminding myself how dangerous he really was.

"Your certainty that you're equipped to handle any injury or emergency that may take place during a rugby training session," he clarified. "When you have no true idea of the complexity of cases we'll be faced with."

"I have a reasonable idea," I said. Where did he get off being a dick? "I did my practical training here, and I've been following the code all my life." I stuck to a respectful tone, colleague to colleague, but wished I knew what Atlas was going to say about him. I should have insisted he tell us, regardless of the chance of being overheard.

Skinner gave me a look down his nose like I was saying I'd graduated to pencil, having previously only been allowed to write with crayons. Maybe he was right, I didn't have the experience he had, but I wasn't clueless either.

"I see," he said slowly. "Well, that makes *all* the difference."

What did he want me to say? Would he have preferred it if I said I wasn't ready, or was incompetent? Because I sure as hell wasn't going to say either of those things. I was mindful of Atlas' warning, but he seemed determined to make me feel like shit.

"I realise I'm new at this," I conceded, "but I am a

fully qualified medical doctor. If an injury occurs, I'm confident I can manage it. If I can't, I'll be sure to ask for your assistance. Assuming you're not too busy to give it."

His eyes narrowed. "If you're going to be difficult, I might have to have a word with the GM about your employment."

Was he threatening me? If he thought I'd be intimidated, he was wrong. Even if it got me fired, I wasn't going to let him walk all over me.

"I'm not trying to be difficult," I said, aware how tight my voice was. "You're the one who called my credentials into question. Frankly, I find that unprofessional. I have a great deal of respect for Doctor Stuart, and for you and your experience." I was toeing a line here, but I wasn't going to roll over for him, or anyone.

"As you should," he said. "Between us, we have a great deal of it. I would have hoped to have more of it on the team." In other words, he would have chosen one of the other candidates for the position. One Bruce might have preferred.

"I guess you're one of those people who expect someone to have experience without being given a chance to do the job," I said dryly. Apparently my last fuck of the day was gone now. I made a note to stock a few extra for next time. Or not, because I didn't owe him anything.

"Experience is great, but it's not everything," I said. "That's why Doctor Stuart hired me. Dominic King agrees with him. They're both willing to give me a chance to prove myself." Let him think that by dropping King's name, maybe I was working with him too, outside of the team. He might back off a bit then.

A girl could hope.

"As am I," Skinner said. "I asked if you were capable of observing training, did I not?"

"You did," I agreed. "And I agreed I am." I glanced at my watch. "Which I'm going to be late for if I don't get going."

I had six or seven minutes to get downstairs and out onto the field. Coach Stanley might wait, not wanting the guys to train without a medic present, but I didn't want to put him in that position. Especially not when I barely started working here. Keeping him waiting would definitely *not* be a good look.

"Turning up for training late would be unprofessional," he said, as if he wasn't the one holding me up. "But better you turn up late with humility, than on time with an overly large ego."

I bit back an angry response and forced a couple of breaths in and out. "I don't have a large ego, Doctor Skinner. I have confidence in my abilities, that's all. And like I said, if I get stuck, I'll call you to help me."

"You did say that," he said. "Right before you accused me of indifference."

What was this guy's deal? Everything I said, he twisted around backward. If I suggested the sky was blue, he'd find a way to prove me wrong. Or try to make me feel bad about being right.

I quickly counted to ten in my head, trying to regain some semblance of calm before I lost my shit with him.

"I didn't mean to accuse you of anything," I said. "I know you care about the players. I know you're passionate about developing new methods to help them regain and maintain their fitness. I'm passionate about that too. I got angry and I spoke without thinking. I'll do my best to make sure that doesn't happen too often."

I wasn't going to promise it wouldn't happen ever again. If he kept pushing me like this, chances were it would.

"You have to be here long enough for it to happen again," he said.

Was he threatening me again?

"I plan on being here for a long time," I said firmly. "Maybe even longer than you."

I was tempted to suggest he'd retire long before I even *thought* about working somewhere else, but he'd most likely take offence at the implied dig at his age. It seemed like I managed to give him enough ammunition as it was. I didn't want to give him any more.

"We'll see," he said. He didn't look convinced. His mouth was set in a firm line and his eyes were cold. A vein in the side of his forehead visibly throbbed, a sign of his annoyance.

Frankly, I didn't give a shit. If this was his attitude toward his co-workers, that was his problem. I'd do my best to be polite and keep the peace around here. I'd definitely do my best not to let him provoke me. If Atlas was wary of him, then who knew what he was capable of?

"If you'll excuse me, I better get down to training," I said.

"Miss Miller," he said after I took a couple of steps away.

I stopped but barely glanced over my shoulder.

"If I was you, I'd watch myself," he said. "You must know our jobs are very sought after. Competition is fierce. Even with the positions filled, people will be after them. Some would take great steps to take the place of one of us. Perhaps all of us. They'd want to prove their experience does, in fact, matter more than your enthusiasm."

I turned around slowly, well and truly done with him, and this conversation.

"That's Doctor Miller." Heels clicking on the floor, I walked out of the infirmary before I said something I'd really regret.

My irritation must have been obvious, because the moment I stepped out onto the side of the field, Frost trotted over to me.

"You okay?" he asked. "Did Atlas—" He looked over to where the inside centre was warming up with the rest.

"He didn't do anything," I said quickly. "I will be fine. When I get a chance to cool down."

Briefly, I told him about the conversation with Otis Skinner. Quietly I added, "Don't kill him. It's nothing I can't deal with."

I was starting to sound like a broken record having to continuously remind the guys not to kill whoever I was talking about. They probably didn't need the constant reminder.

Or, maybe they did. They all seemed very ready to act on my behalf, whether I liked it or not.

I corrected my previous thought that I'd gone

from dating rugby players to mafia spies. More accurately, I'd gone from dating football players to dating hitmen.

Some women would kill to be in my position. It wasn't that I didn't appreciate it, it just put me on edge much of the time.

I'd seen a lot of things in Dusk Bay, things they wouldn't have dreamt of. They might think life here was glamorous, but the reality was dark and covered in blood. And when it had you, it gripped you, unwilling to let you go.

Should I have looked for a job somewhere else? I could have hidden out in a club in Ireland or Scotland. Somewhere further from the violence.

Could I have done that? No, I wouldn't have. When it came down to it, this was home. As hard as I tried to deny the darkness, I was the one who pulled a gun on Belinda Simmons. I was the one who gave her the death sentence, even if I didn't slide the blade in.

Whether I wanted it or not, I was part of this life. More and more, it sucked me back in.

"Now you sound like Storm," he said with a smile. He nodded over to where the fullback was doing warm up stretches. "Usually when he's dealing with Atlas."

I snorted softly. "Trust me, Otis Skinner is nothing like Atlas. He's more prickly than an echidna, but he keeps it covered with his mask of professional distance." And he had the nerve to accuse *me* of being arrogant.

"You're right, that doesn't sound anything like Atlas," Frost agreed. "He's definitely not distant. If anything, he's more the in-your-face type."

"It's one of the things I like about him," I said.

"Me too," Frost agreed. "Remind me not to get injured when Skinner is around. He doesn't sound like the kind of doctor I want to treat me."

"He's a good doctor," I said reluctantly. "He's just not a nice person."

"He could learn a thing or two from you and your brother," Frost said.

"My brother would be only too happy to teach him," I said wryly.

I shouldn't imagine Otis Skinner chained up in Ice's workroom, but the mental image was in my brain before I could stop it. I wish I could say I didn't like it, but I was so annoyed right now, it fit in perfectly with my mood.

"So would I," Frost said, after glancing around to make sure no one was listening. A few of the coaching staff stood several metres away, each engaged in conversation, discussing plays and training tactics. They weren't paying us any attention.

"Don't," I warned. "Atlas said to keep an eye out for him. Let's not provoke him." Like I had. I'd have to watch my back around him.

"Who's provoking?" he asked. "I think of it as dealing with someone who has you upset." He put an arm around my waist and pulled me to him.

I resisted for a moment, but then let him draw me closer. Anyone who looked at us would see I was ruffled. He was a friend comforting me, that was all. And if people wanted to see anything more, they would anyway just by watching us talk quietly together. If people were good at anything, it was jumping to conclusions. Myself included.

"If you dealt with everyone who upset me, you'd spend all your time doing that," I said. I leaned against him, trying to absorb his warm confidence. I couldn't deny he was sweet for making the offer, because he was, but his desire to turn to violence so quickly was still a little chilling.

"Retirement doesn't seem so bad." He chuckled.

"How about you go and warm up with the rest of the guys?" I suggested. "Otherwise you might be forced to retire from an injury caused by not warming up properly. Also, Coach Stanley is looking at you like you better get your ass out there." The last thing I needed was to get in trouble for sidetracking him.

"Only because I don't want to get in trouble with my doctor." He kissed my forehead and dropped his arm from me. "I'll see you soon."

I nodded and watched him trot away, quietly wishing this day was over already.

Chapter Sixteen

Chelsea

"WHAT THE HELL IS HE DOING HERE?"

I glanced over to Storm, who half-held the door open.

Atlas shouldered past him, Ramsey right behind. Neither seemed intimidated by the big fullback.

"He's part of this." Atlas moved to stand beside Jay, who was equally unruffled.

Clearly he knew why Ramsey was here too. He shifted his shoulders uncomfortably when the other guys approached. As though there were suddenly too many people in the room.

Even without being on the spectrum, I understood. These guys each had a presence that sucked the air from the room. With all of them here, becoming overwhelmed was easy.

I trusted if Jay needed to step aside, he would. We'd understand if he did. He had to do what was necessary to take care of himself. Like everyone else here did. If we were going to be any kind of family, we'd have to learn to understand each other and support everyone's needs.

Ramsey shrugged and stepped over to help himself to one of the bowls of salmon and salad that sat on the kitchen island. He sat on the back of the couch and started to eat like he owned the place.

I hadn't ever seen him quite so relaxed. The opposite of everyone else. The tension was so thick I could have touched it.

Frost smiled, but he still looked tense.

Dallas looked like he wished this was over with. I could relate to that sentiment.

Storm glared at the newcomers, but closed and locked the door before he picked up his bowl.

"I'll make one more," I said.

Hand shaking with anxiety, I spooned more salad and fish into a seventh bowl and grabbed another fork to sit inside it.

The food looked good, but I wasn't hungry. Between the run-in with Otis Skinner, and anticipation of what Atlas was going to tell us, I was full of nerves.

It also wasn't lost on me that I was surrounded by testosterone. So much of it. Each of the guys were attractive in his own way. Each different from the last. Dark and brooding, light and cheerful, but all with an edge of danger that drew me in more and more every day.

I was a butterfly caught in a web, surrounded by spiders. All of who might just want to eat me alive. I wasn't even trying to struggle to get away. I was happy to spread my wings and let myself be consumed.

In some ways, that was the most terrifying thing of all.

"Start talking," Storm said to Atlas. He waved his fork at him to hurry up.

"Are you sure it's safe here?" Atlas looked around, scrutinising the room. Searching for hidden cameras and listening devices. Or ones that weren't hidden.

I looked carefully too, but I hadn't seen any. According to my brother, this place should be as secure as Storm suggested it was. If it wasn't, we'd find out the hard way.

"It better be," Storm growled. "Stop fucking around and tell us what's going on. Are you working for Dominic King?" His tone was direct, blunt. He wanted all the answers and he wanted them right this minute. He wasn't the most patient person in the first place, and clearly he'd run out of every last remaining fuck.

Atlas met his gaze, unwavering. "No," he said firmly. "The opposite. I work for the Brantley family. I have for a long time. When King started making his move, they wanted me to keep an eye on him. They knew he had his eyes on Dusk Bay. At least, they suspected he did." He rolled his lips, brow creased in thought.

"So you killed Bruce Fergus, allowing him the in he was looking for," Storm concluded. He scratched the centre of his brow with his thumbnail, trying to get his head around everything. This clearly wasn't going the way he expected. He obviously wasn't ready to believe anything Atlas, or the other two, said. Not yet.

"I told you why I killed him," Atlas replied evenly. "Because he would have hired someone else instead of Chelsea. But I had approval to do it, for the reason you said. If it wasn't me, it would have been someone else. Probably King himself."

"What does that have to do with you playing for the Smashers?" It was Frost who asked.

"They wanted Jay and I in place before he made

his move," Atlas said. "We might have..." He glanced over to Jay. "We might have objected to being sent here. Where we were, it was good for our careers. But we were given no choice." He shrugged. "We were also told to figure out which of the guys would be recruited."

"You recruited Ramsey?" I asked. My gaze swivelled to him, then back to Atlas.

Ramsey snorted. "Nope."

"He was already working for the Brantley family," Atlas supplied. "He was our first contact on the team. We got our orders through him."

I raised my eyebrows at Ramsey, who raised his back at me. I should have seen that coming. Someone who doesn't say much, who blends into the background, what else would he be?

"So, we're all working on the same side," Frost concluded. He seemed both relieved and pleased at the idea. Of course he was, this changed everything and made his attraction to Atlas a lot easier to swallow. So to speak. Also may be literally.

"Exactly." Atlas snagged up a bowl of salad and stabbed a piece of lettuce before pushing it into his mouth.

"You didn't think to mention any of this to us?" Storm asked.

"You weren't friendly," Ramsey said. He wasn't accusing, not exactly, just stating a fact.

"And they weren't working with us until recently," Jay added. "We didn't know if we could trust them." He clearly trusted Atlas and Ramsey.

"I'm so glad we don't have to kill you," Frost said, gesturing to all three of them.

"I'm *mostly* relieved about that too," Atlas said. He glanced sidelong at Storm.

Storm glared back at him. "If I haven't mentioned it lately, fuck off. Just because we're on the same side doesn't mean we have to be friends. I haven't decided if I trust you yet."

"Same to you," Atlas said. "You haven't given me any reason to."

Storm grunted. "You can talk. It wasn't a stretch to think you killed Bruce so your boss could take his job. How do we really know that's not what happened?"

"Because I'm telling you it isn't," Atlas said. "If you don't believe me, there's plenty of people you can ask. Daisy Lasalle, for one. Gianni. Hell, go ask Reuben Brantley himself if it'll make you feel better. They'll all back up what I told you."

Storm looked over to me.

"I can check with Daze." I was going to have to,

because I suspected he wouldn't believe Atlas until someone like her confirmed it. Otherwise, we'd spend all night going back and forth, both guys trying to take verbal bites out of each other. Or maybe literal ones. Storm had a whole drawer full of sharp knives. For cooking, but it wouldn't take much for the situation to escalate out of hand.

"Do it," Storm said.

I slid my phone over the countertop to me, and tapped on the screen before holding it to my ear. While hoping like hell she didn't mind me calling out of the blue.

"Hey," she said when the call connected.

I waited for her to say more, but she didn't.

I cleared my throat. "I'm sorry to bother you, but I'm here with Atlas Underwood, Jay Lang and Ferris Ramsey." I chewed my lip and waited for her response. People didn't just ring up Daisy Lasalle for a friendly chat. Chances were, I'd owe her favour just because she answered. It might take years for her to ask for payment, but she would. I was very, very certain of that.

She laughed. "Oh, I've been waiting for this conversation."

"You have?" I eyed the guys.

They all looked back at me, wondering what

Daze was saying in my ear. My nerves quickly doubled. Maybe we should have gone to see her face to face, instead of calling her. That would have meant arranging a meeting, and doing that would have taken time. Assuming she'd agree to it at all. She was a busy woman; she didn't have to bother with everyone who wanted a few moments' conversation with her.

She continued. "Atlas told me about the team, and how they didn't trust him and Jay. After Dominic King arrived in town, closely followed by Otis Skinner, it wasn't difficult to figure out how coincidental that would look. It's not. We had plans in place for a long time. Even to the point of encouraging Bruce to retire. What Atlas did pushed things forward a little faster than we planned, but we wanted King where we could keep an eye on him. And we're relying on you to do exactly that."

"And by 'you,' you mean—" I winced.

"All of you," she said firmly. "Including you, Chelsea. I know you don't want to be involved, but you are. You're in the perfect position to keep an eye on both of them, Skinner in particular. I know you won't let me down."

I winced harder. "I don't really think—"

"I'm not giving you a choice, Chelsea," she said,

her voice bordering on stone cold. She could be tougher than nails when she wanted to be. "You can do what I'm asking you to do, or we'll find you somewhere else to work. Somewhere you might not enjoy as much as you enjoy working for the Smashers."

I swallowed. There was no doubt in my mind she meant exactly what she said. If I didn't do what she wanted, she'd shove me out of the way. Without a second thought. If doing that pissed off anyone, including my brother, she'd have them dealt with.

"Do we understand each other?" she asked.

"Ye—" My voice squeaked. I tried again. "Yes, we understand each other."

"I thought we did." Her voice softened like she was smiling through the phone. "I know you'll do a wonderful job. You and all of those boys. It looks like you're going to have your hands full."

"I guess so," I said. All I wanted now was to end the conversation. "Thank you for clearing everything up."

"Any time," she said sweetly. "You can take any orders that come from Ramsey as coming from me."

I glanced up and met his gaze. He looked back at me like he was amused in some way. Right now, I couldn't get my head around why that might be.

"Okay," I said, glancing down at the kitchen island.

"Are the rest of the guys with you?" Daze asked.

"Storm Keller, Daniel Frost and Dallas Gregory are here," I confirmed. My gaze skimmed from one to the other as I said their names.

Storm frowned, but the other two seemed curious. Whatever was going down, they were ready for it.

"Good, you can tell them what I just told you," she said. "I expect all of you to keep an eye on Dominic King and Otis Skinner. And anyone else they bring in from the Sydney Devils. Players, staff, whatever. I don't care if it's the person who cleans the toilets. They're planning something and I want to know what it is long before it happens."

Even though she couldn't see me, I nodded. "We will. Nothing will get past us." I hoped like hell that was true.

"Make sure it doesn't," she said. "I'm sure you'll understand what will happen if it does."

"Yes," I said. "We'll die."

Chapter Seventeen

Dallas

I SAT ON THE COUCH BESIDE CHELSEA, MY ARM around her. She nestled into me, breathing soft and low. Awake, but relaxed.

"Well, that was interesting," Frost said.

Storm grunted. He hadn't said a word since the other three guys left. He sat in an armchair finishing his dinner while brooding, lost in thought.

"It was," I agreed. "I told you they were good guys." I hadn't exactly, but close enough.

"Just because they're on our side doesn't mean they're good guys," Storm grunted.

"It does if it means Atlas killed Bruce for Chelsea," Frost said. "It sounds like something out of a movie." He cocked his head and smiled.

"I wish he'd taken the retirement option," Chelsea said softly. "He'd still be alive if he had."

"And Dominic King would have been GM for longer," I concluded. "Maybe before Atlas and Jay joined the team. What would that have meant?"

"Maybe nothing," Storm said. "Maybe something."

"King might have stopped them from joining the team," Frost suggested.

We all stared at him.

"Fuck," Storm said softly.

"What?" Chelsea sat up a little and covered her yawn with her fist.

"We don't know what Dominic King knows about Atlas and the rest of us," Storm said. "He could know exactly what we're up to."

She stiffened in my arms. "Shit." After a moment, she loosened a little and shook her head. "I didn't get that impression from him or Skinner. They might suspect there's people like us watching them, but I don't think they know who. If they did, they would have pulled strings to have Atlas and Jay stay at the Devils. Or go somewhere else."

"I hope you're right," Storm said. "Otherwise we've just been thrown into a tank full of hungry sharks. I'm not going to be their fucking bait."

"We won't end up bait," I said. "We'll be fine."

"And taking orders from Ramsey." Frost seemed amused by that. "Who would have thought?"

"Not me," I agreed. "Storm, are you going to do what he says?" I was poking the hornet's nest, but I couldn't resist. If anyone was going to make this situation difficult, it was him.

"We'll see," he grunted. "Depends what they want. If he tells me to kill any one of you, he can fuck all the way off."

"The only way he'd have to ask you to do that is if one of us does something wrong," Chelsea said.

"Then we won't do anything wrong," I said.

I was starting to wonder what we let ourselves get sucked into. What would happen if we packed up everything right now and slipped away into the night? I suspected I wouldn't like the repercussions. People like our new employers, they had long memories and longer reach. Atlas, Jay and Ramsey might hunt us down. Holed up in a warehouse somewhere, waiting for them to break down the door and kill us all.

"Piece of cake," Frost said. "We know how to stay out of trouble if we want to."

"Trouble has a way of finding us," Chelsea said softly.

I pulled her in closer. "I know you didn't want to get caught up in all of this. If I could have done anything to prevent it, I would have." I don't know what I would have done, but I would have tried something.

She sighed. "I know. If it wasn't this, it would have been something else. If it wasn't you guys, it would have been some*one* else. They've always been determined to find a way to bring me back in. That's what they're like. They don't like letting anyone go."

"Has that ever happened?" Frost asked. "Does anyone get to walk away?"

"Once in a while someone is able to find a way to break free," she said. "If they can cut a deal with the right person at the right time, they can live a normal life. But it doesn't happen often. Some people are used without even knowing it's happening. Others, like me, they wait for an opportunity to hold on to me. To make me do whatever they want." She sounded frustrated, but resigned. She didn't want this, but she knew she couldn't fight it.

"I don't like the idea of anyone manipulating you." Storm scowled.

She laughed softly. "They're manipulating all of us. It's what they do. There's three things they want in life: power, money and control. As far as they're concerned, those three are all rolled into one. With one comes the others. They don't like to relinquish a centimetre or a cent. The more power and control they have, the more they want."

She nestled tighter against me. "Daze likes me, but she'd have me killed if necessary and not think twice about it, especially if she thought I gave her a reason to do it. She's as ruthless as the rest of them."

"What about Ice?" Frost asked. "He wouldn't let her do that to you."

"No, he wouldn't," she agreed. "There's six people he wouldn't let her kill: me, Kennedy, Mannix, Ares, and our parents. If anyone went after us, they'd either have to get past him, or get to us before he could stop them. And face the consequences of pissing him off. Chances are, they'd kill him before they went after me, so he couldn't do anything to stop them."

"Rugby is starting to feel very passive in comparison," Storm remarked.

"Are you starting to regret getting involved?" Frost frowned at him.

Storm shrugged one shoulder and leaned back against the back of the chair. "Doesn't matter, does it? We're in now."

"Because I got you in," Chelsea said regretfully. "I shouldn't have told you anything."

"We were in when I wrapped my hands around Ivy's throat," Frost said. "At least, I was. When your brother helped me, I was all in."

"And if Frost is in, I'm in," Storm said.

"I'm in because I decided to be," I said. "But I'm in even more now Chelsea is. If Dominic King or Otis Skinner try anything with her, I'm going to take a leaf from Storm's book and rip off their hand to smack them with it."

"I bet Ice would literally do that," Frost said. He seemed to have a genuine case of hero worship.

"He would," Chelsea agreed. "I'm sure if you ask nicely, he'll let you try it out sometime."

She looked less than enthusiastic. If someone wrote a book about her, they could call it *Reluctant Mafia Princess*. She was a princess, whether she liked it or not and I wasn't going to let anything happen to her, even if I had to die to prevent it.

"I don't know if that's fun or just fucked up," Storm said.

"Both?" Frost suggested.

Chelsea shook her head slightly, making her hair fall across her face. "I vote for fucked up, but if that's what you're into..."

"Not me," I said. "I'm not as bloodthirsty as those two. I just want to keep you safe. Anything else is shit that has to be done."

"You say that until you actually kill someone," Frost said, his voice low, almost hypnotic. "When you get a taste of it, you might find you like it more than you thought you would."

"I might," I said. "I might not. I might not ever find out."

"I hope you don't," Chelsea said. "I don't want any of you killing for me. Or killing for shits and giggles. It's not a thing anyone should do lightly."

"Have you killed people?" Frost asked, looking a bit too eager.

"Not directly," she said. "Apparently I excel at doing it indirectly. Belinda Simmons. Bruce Fergus. I can't help feeling responsible for Ivy too. She might have come on to Frost because she saw him with me. Because she couldn't handle me having something good that she didn't. She wanted him for herself. I don't know why, but she couldn't understand that what she had was special, her looks and her talent. She didn't need to be me."

"No offence to her, but no one is you," I said. "If she couldn't see that, that was her problem."

I was sympathetic for the girl and the way she

died, but anyone comparing themselves to Chelsea was in for a world of disappointment. No one was as beautiful, smart and sexy as her. No one would ever taste as good. No one made better sounds when they came.

"I know," she said. "Still..."

"It might be my fault for being irresistible." Frost pretended to fluff his hair. "She saw me and had to have me. Can you blame her?"

"Lucky you're cute," Storm told him. "Because sometimes you're an idiot." He said it with affection, but at the same time rolled his eyes and smirked.

"Only sometimes?" I teased.

Frost flipped me off, then did the same to Storm. "I'm very cute. Right Chelsea?"

"Right," she agreed. "You're all adorable. I don't know what I'd do without you."

"You'll never have to find out," I assured her. "So, what happens now? With Atlas and Jay. Ramsey too, I guess."

"Yeah, Storm doesn't have any reason to try to chase them away anymore," Frost said.

"I do," Storm said. "Atlas is still a dickhead. The jury is out on Jay and Ramsey. But I've already given them permission to be involved with Chelsea, so this changes nothing. As it stands, there *seems* to be slightly less chance they'll try to screw us over. Only slightly."

"I can't wait until you and Atlas are best friends," Frost said. "Then you might admit you're wrong about him."

He regarded Storm, something like hope in his green eyes. He was as invested in this family as I was. He wanted everyone to get along and care about each other. He was like a kid who wanted all his friends to sit down together and play with Legos. Or have a game of Monopoly without anyone tossing the board onto the floor. If that was even possible.

Did people really do that? I had no idea. I wasn't a fan of the game, so I had little interest in finding out. Especially not with these guys. They were so competitive, they'd do anything to win. Things would get ugly, to say the least.

"Never," Storm said.

"You're never going to be best friends, or you'll never admit to being wrong?" I asked.

He eyed me. "Both. The best you can hope for is for us to tolerate each other. Don't go expecting anything else to happen."

I wondered what it would take to change his mind. Atlas didn't seem like a bad guy to me, they just butted heads. What was it Ramsey said? Alpha men. They both wanted power and control and didn't want to give it to the other. Sooner or later, something was going to have to give. Someone was going to have to bend a little. If not, we might all break.

"I bet you fifty bucks," Frost said to me.

"What timeframe?" I asked. Years could pass before they learned to like each other.

Frost tapped the tips of his fingers against his cheek as he thought. "Two months? I bet fifty dollars Storm and Atlas will be friends within two months."

"That's a dumbass bet," Storm told him. He scowled at us both and shook his head like he thought we were out of our minds. He might be right, but neither of us gave a shit.

I leaned over and shook Frost's hand. "It'll be the easiest fifty bucks I ever make." I wouldn't mind if I lost, because that would mean our family was a little less dysfunctional. Either way, I won.

Frost grinned. "How much do you want to bet within six months they'll be sucking each other's cocks?"

Chapter Eighteen

Chelsea

I woke like I had so many times recently, with Dallas' cock still deep inside me. Apart from taking a couple of breaks to use the toilet, we'd been like that all night. Every time one of us would slip back to bed, we'd fuck again and fall asleep like that.

"Morning," he said sleepily.

"Morning," I said back.

I brushed hair out of my eyes and looked over to his face, his eyes bleary. He looked particularly adorable like that. A smoking hot wall of muscle who was vulnerable for the first minutes of each day, before he fully woke up.

Same with the other two guys. Storm in particular. This was the only time he let down his guard.

When he was asleep, or half asleep. He always caught up faster than the others. coming fully awake and putting his shields back in place.

"Did you sleep well?" He stroked the back of his hand down the side of my cheek. his hips started to move, slowly thrusting his cock in and out of me. Of course he was hard again.

I never met anyone who was so hard, so often. Knowing I did that to him made my body throb in response. He was constantly aroused because of me. And I was constantly aroused because of him and the other guys.

"I slept pretty well," I said. I half-closed my eyes and savoured the feeling of him moving inside me. At the same time, I was aware of Frost and Storm waking slowly. It was a tight fit, but the bed was big enough for the four of us to sleep. As long as no one stretched out like a starfish. Then they could look forward to an elbow or a knee in the offending limb.

"Whatever stamina pills you're taking, I want some," Frost said.

He popped his head up over my shoulder, so I could see him in the corner of my eye.

Dallas glanced up at him. "No pills, just Chelsea. I don't need anything else to get me going."

"Good point," Frost said. "She does have that effect on all of us. Right, Stormy?"

Predictably, Storm grunted. "Yep. So do you. Why don't you get over here and suck my cock?"

"I was waiting to be invited," Frost said.

"You don't need to be invited," Storm said. "Just dive right in."

"I'll remember that for next time." Frost's face disappeared under the covers.

I rolled Dallas and me over so I was straddling his hips. That gave me a better view of Storm, his eyes rolling back in his head in pleasure. He pushed the covers aside, revealing Frost, his mouth covering Storm's cock.

I was already aroused, but seeing that made me even hotter. I loved that they cared about each other and wanted to be physical with each other. The bond between them was becoming tighter and tighter because of it. In turn, that was bringing our little family closer together. And watching them was better than any porn ever made.

"Like what you see?" Storm asked, looking at me through one open eye.

"I like it very much," I said. I could have watched it all day.

"It feels fucking good," Storm said on a sigh.

"Tastes good," Frost said, lifting his mouth off Storm's for long enough to speak.

Storm eyed him. "I bet your ass feels good too." It was as tentative as I'd ever seen him. Not willing to be pushy for once. This was something that, if they did it, Frost would have to be completely on board. Otherwise, it wouldn't happen. At least, not today.

In typical Frost fashion, the blonde prop smiled. "I bet it does. Do you want to find out?"

"Hell yeah, I do," Storm agreed. He rolled his upper body over just enough to open the drawer beside the bed and pull out the tube of lube we kept in there.

At this point, we might as well keep it on top of the table. He opened the lid and gestured for Frost to roll over onto his side.

While I slowly rode Dallas, I watched Storm squirt lube onto the tips of two fingers and smear them carefully over Frost's rear hole.

Frost lay still, except for his eyes, which rolled around, looking at me, then trying to look at Storm. "You will be gentle with me, won't you?" he asked.

"Nope." Storm tossed the lube back onto the

table and pried Frost's butt cheeks apart before pushing a finger slowly into him. Gently and carefully.

He put it on that he was a big, bad asshole, but when it came down to it, he knew how to be loving, even sensitive. Nothing he'd ever admit to, of course but it was there for the three of us to see.

"How does that feel?" I asked Frost. I knew how it felt for me, but he might feel differently. Not everyone liked anal.

"It feels like heaven," Frost said. "Different, but nice. I want more." He said the last over his shoulder to Storm.

"Then I'll give you more," Storm told him. He pressed another finger inside Frost's ass.

Frost's eyes half-closed and the corners of his mouth tipped up in a smile. "Why didn't I do this sooner?"

"Because I wasn't ready for you," Storm told him.

Frost twisted around to raise his eyebrows at him and shake his head. "Of course, why didn't I think of that?"

"Because you need me to do the thinking for you," Storm teased.

"I'd tell you to fuck off, but that feels too good."

Frost lay back down. "Is this where I have to beg you for your cock?"

"Definitely," Storm agreed. He slid his fingers in and out of Frost's well-lubricated hole. "If you want more, you're going to have to plead your case."

Frost, who now gripped his own cock with his hand, made a face. "I don't think I have enough blood in the head on my shoulders to have a coherent conversation, much less give you three good reasons to fuck my ass."

"I wasn't asking for three," Storm told him. "I'll settle for one, but you better make it good."

"Because I want you to?" Frost suggested. "Because if you don't, I'll lose my mind? Because my ass is going to be nice and tight, since no one has ever fucked me there before?"

"That was three," Dallas pointed out.

Frost grinned. "It was, wasn't it? Go me." He glanced back at Storm. "How about it?"

Storm groaned. "You had me at no one has fucked you there before." He pulled out his fingers and positioned his cock in their place.

Frost tensed as though expecting it to hurt, but his eyes widened as Storm slowly, slowly pushed himself inside. At first, just his tip, but gradually more as Frost relaxed, taking him in. Letting him slide in deeper and deeper.

"Holy hell, you're fucking tight," Storm whispered.

"I don't want to do that, but it's hot to watch," Dallas said. He thrusted up into me harder and faster, but still unhurried.

"It definitely is," I said, rubbing my clit on him just a bit more, creating extra friction. It also opened up more possibilities of things we could do. Things we could explore later.

"I've decided you're right," Storm said to Frost. "Why didn't we do this sooner?"

"Because you both need me to think for you," Dallas said quickly.

Storm snorted. "You have a hard enough time thinking as it is. Can you think about anything other than fucking Chelsea?"

"Why would I want to?" Dallas asked. "What else is there in life? Fucking and football."

"He has a point." Frost had his eyes closed, stroking himself while Storm thrust in and out of his ass. "Kinda. I don't know if footy is as good as this. It might be time to think about retiring and spending my days like this."

"Of course my cock is that amazing you want to give up footy so I can fuck you with it," Storm said.

"That sounds about right," Frost said. "I can think of worse ways to spend the rest of my life."

"Me too," Dallas said softly. "Can we all call in sick today?"

"I wish we could," I said with a sigh. Even if we didn't have to keep an eye on King and Skinner, I hadn't been with the team for long enough to accumulate any sick leave. Not to mention, it wouldn't be a good look after only being there for a short time.

I admit though, it was fucking tempting. Lying in bed all day with these three guys would be the perfect day.

"Another good reason to retire," Frost said. "We wouldn't have to bother calling in sick. We could just do whatever we wanted all day long."

"You'd be bored in a day or two," Storm told him. "Not of fucking, but not getting out out of the house and being active."

"This building has a gym," Frost pointed out. "We could have food delivered. I see no reason to leave." He stroked himself faster, in rhythm with Storm's hips. They were almost matching Dallas and I stroke for stroke; all of us getting faster, closer to coming.

"Let's talk about it later." Storm's face was

strained with effort. Slick with sweat. I could tell by his breathing he was close.

"Is it okay if he comes in your ass?" I asked. I wanted to see that, but it was their choice. Frost in particular.

Storm's brow creased in a brief frown. "Yeah, can I?" He looked annoyed at himself that he hadn't thought to ask first. He'd let himself get lost in the moment and hadn't considered this all the way through.

"Yes, please," Frost said. "I want you to come inside me."

Storm groaned. "Fuck, yeah. Good boy."

Frost eyes widened. "I like that. Being called a good boy."

"You're a very good boy," I told him.

"Chelsea—" Apparently he did like it a lot, because as he said my name, he came, squirting pearly cum over his own fingers.

"Fuck." Storm was right behind him, coming deep and hard inside Frost's ass.

In unison, Dallas and I were right behind them. My pussy tightened around his cock as I came hard, stealing an orgasm from him at the same time. We cried out together, pushing each other harder, milking the bliss for every incredible moment. As if somehow this would be our last time coming together. Both shattering together into a thousand tiny pieces before coming back into our own bodies and sagging together.

"Wow, that was something else," Frost said when he could finally talk again. "I definitely want to do that again."

"You'll definitely be doing that again," Storm told him. "I'm going to wear out your ass and Chelsea's pussy. And both of your mouths."

"If you'll let me, I'll wear yours out too," Frost said, his voice low with uncertainty and a tinge of need. Scared Storm might say no. Hoping like hell he didn't.

"We can wear each other out," Storm said after a moment of hesitation.

He carefully pulled out of Frost and wrapped his arms around the other man, holding him close and speaking without words. He was falling head over heels for Frost, if he hadn't already.

I knew without doubt Frost felt the same way. I was happy for them. Both of them together were fucking adorable. I was honoured to be a part of their lives and family.

I hoped like hell they'd let the other guys in. Right now, I felt like I lived two lives: one with these guys, another with Atlas and Jay. I had a date with them tonight, but I'd have to find a chance for all of us to get together. For them to all get to know each other. One thing at a time.

Right now, the separation gave me a chance to get to know the other two with fewer interruptions and pressure. If we were lucky, and careful, we had plenty of time for more.

Chapter Nineteen

Chelsea

"Is this where you tell me you won't say where we're going?" I stepped around a crack in the sidewalk and gave Atlas and Jay a curious look.

"I like surprises," Atlas said.

"I don't," Jay said. "Where are we going?" He stuck his jaw forward, and glared at Atlas. A hint of a smile tugged at the corners of his mouth.

"Can you be patient for once?" Atlas asked. Impatiently.

"Nope," Jay replied.

"What he said," I agreed. In a loud, conspiratorial whisper I asked Jay, "Should we threaten to tickle him or something?"

Jay grinned. "I know exactly where he's ticklish."

"I know where you keep your socks," Atlas told him. "I could put spiders in them."

Jay bumped his shoulder against Atlas'. "Go ahead. That'll give me an excuse not to wear them." He wore canvas shoes without socks, even though the evening was cool.

"You laugh now, but they'll crawl into your underwear drawer and start breeding," Atlas said.

"Then I won't wear underwear either," Jay said easily.

He looked over to me. It was his turn to whisper loudly, "He thinks he's good at making threats. You might've noticed, he's pretty shit." He smiled warmly at me and Atlas.

"Only because I wasn't making threats," Atlas said simply. "If I was making an actual threat, it'd be better than that."

"Are you going to give us an example?" I asked. This banter between us was nice. A break from the tension of the last couple of days.

"I would, but I don't want to scare you," Atlas said.

I snorted. "You'd have to try pretty hard to scare me. When it comes to threats, I've probably seen and heard them all."

"You could teach Atlas," Jay said, elbowing the

inside centre. "The last time he tried to get to someone, he put confetti in their locker."

"It was their school bag, and I was seven," Atlas said. "I've pulled better pranks than that."

"Name one," Jay said.

Atlas hesitated.

Jay snapped his fingers. "See? You need all the help you can get."

"What about you?" I asked Jay. "What pranks have you pulled?" I'd rather talk about those than actual threats.

"Epic ones." Jay puffed out his chest. "Like the time I put lemon juice in everyone's drinking water."

"Fuck off," Atlas said. "That was you?" He seemed impressed, eyes wider with a hint of awe.

"With a bit of help," Jay admitted. "But it was my idea. We should pull that on Storm. It would be awesome."

I tried to bite back a laugh, but failed. "I shouldn't encourage you, but I'd like to see the expression on his face." Although, that would likely be followed by Storm living up to his name. The aftermath might not be worth the giggle.

"You should definitely encourage us," Atlas said. "Most of the pranks we pull are harmless."

"'Most of them,' he says." I grimaced at him. "What about the ones that aren't?"

"One of the Devils players put itching powder in the coach's shoes right before he was about to put them on," Jay said. "Turned out, he was allergic to it. His feet blew up like balloons and stayed like that for about a week. He was really pissed off and uncomfortable. They could have ended up worse."

"They never found who did it." Atlas gave Jay a sidelong look.

The look Jay gave him back was pure innocence. "They can't prove anything."

"I wouldn't have picked either of you for pranksters," I said.

"Some of the Smashers don't share our sense of humour," Atlas said. "With the animosity on the team, it was better to keep our heads down. Let them get used to us."

"And vice versa," I said. "Now they have, can I look forward to hearing stories about glitter in places glitter shouldn't go."

"Glitter is evil," Jay said, with a mock shudder. "You wouldn't catch me pranking anyone with glitter."

"They wouldn't *catch* you," I echoed. "That

doesn't mean you wouldn't do it." Yeah, I was onto him.

Jay grinned. "If I was to use it, I'd exercise discretion."

"No using it on Dominic King or Otis Skinner," Atlas said. "Unless you and your glitter want a shallow grave."

"Hell no," Jay agreed. "I wouldn't prank Chelsea with it either." He took my hand and held it loosely in his.

"It's nice to know I'm safe from glitter," I said dryly. "What worries me is what not I'm not safe from. You're not going to put thumbtacks on my work chair, are you? Or bring me coffee that has salt instead of sugar? Or put icing on a sponge, pretending it's cake?"

"No, but those are all good ideas," Jay said. "Which one of those have you done?"

"Jay Lang, did you just suggest I'd prank someone? Like, my teachers at school?" I pretended to be outraged.

"You did, didn't you?" Atlas asked, ending the question with a laugh. "I bet you raised hell when you were at school."

"Not really," I said. "I was the one who sat quietly

and got my work done. Which is why they never figured out I made the fake cake."

After they both had a good laugh, I added, "That particular teacher was mean. She used to hold the whole class back during lunchtime if one kid did anything wrong. I tried to explain to her that it wasn't fair to punish all of us because one person decided to be a dickhead. She gave me detention, and kept on doing what she was doing."

She was lucky she wasn't around these days, or she could look forward to spending some time with my brother. Which was extreme, even given the way she treated us.

"Sounds like one of my teachers," Jay said ruefully. "He used to get angry at me for being distracted in class. Problem was, I knew the work already and I was bored. Or I didn't understand why we needed to know it. I can focus if I give a shit."

"It sounded like he needed more training," I said. It must be difficult to teach a class full of kids who all had different learning abilities and interests, but no one should be punished for being bored, or if the work wasn't challenging enough.

"Yeah, I guess so." Jay shrugged. "Anyway, Atlas has sidetracked us enough. He was just about to tell us where we're going." He looked over to Atlas, his head tilted sideways.

"No I wasn't," Atlas said. "But you can see it up ahead."

Jay and I both looked.

"Demons' Arena?" I asked. "It's not hockey season yet." Which was a shame, because I would have enjoyed seeing a game with them.

"I know," Atlas said. "Otherwise we'd have seats at the front, right behind the plexiglass. I buy season tickets every year."

"He's slightly obsessed with hockey," Jay said.

"If I wasn't playing footy, I'd be an ice hockey player," Atlas said.

"I'd be a sprinter," Jay said. "Rugby is the only team sport I ever liked. Everything else, I preferred to be an individual."

"No one could accuse you of being anything other than an individual," Atlas said affectionately.

"You too," Jay told him. "So, what are we doing at Demons' Arena? Watching preseason training?"

"Huh." Atlas frowned. "I should have thought of that. Good guess, but no."

"We're not taking part in an attack like the one that happened five years ago, are we?" I asked carefully.

So many people died in that attack, it was considered a dark time, even by Dusk Bay standards. Just thinking about it gave me chills. I could easily have been there, watching the game. Thankfully, we didn't go that night, but we heard the horror stories afterwards. That was bad enough.

Atlas pointed a finger gun at me. "Also a good idea, but no. We're not attacking anyone. That is to say, an attack isn't on tonight's agenda, but I'm always open to a change of plan. You never know what might happen around here."

"Let's hope that doesn't happen," I said, giving him a well-deserved side eye.

That wasn't my idea of a fun way to spend the evening. Admittedly, I knew plenty of people who would put that at the top of the list. Strangely, my brother wasn't even one of them. The Brantley twins, definitely, but not him. He preferred a more subtle approach, unless there was no other choice. If there wasn't, he'd take part.

"If it does come, we'll be ready," Jay assured me. He squeezed my hand lightly.

In spite of the contact, he didn't make any effort to bring me any closer to him. If he needed his personal space, I was happy to give it to him. I'd wait for him to decide when and if he wanted more.

"It must be nice to have a normal life." I sighed softly.

"I don't know, normal looks boring to me," Atlas said. "Jay and I usually get restless on a night off."

"Yes, but you don't go and attack people or places because you get bored," I said. "On any given night in Dusk Bay, that could happen."

I couldn't help looking over my shoulder. As far as I could tell, no one followed us. I couldn't see anyone lurking in the shadows, ready to make trouble.

Just because I didn't see them, didn't mean they weren't there though. I wouldn't assume. Assuming anything in this town could get you dead.

"We won't let it happen," Atlas assured me. "Come on, let's get inside." He led us over to a small door at the rear of the building and tapped on it.

After a few moments, the door opened.

"I was starting to think you weren't coming." Coast Riggs, the team's strength and conditioning coach, grinned and held out a hand to Atlas. "This must be Chelsea. They've both said a lot about you." He shook Atlas' hand before offering to shake mine.

I noticed he didn't make the same offer to Jay.

"All good," Jay interjected.

My face heated. "I'm sure they exaggerated."

"They often do, but you're as cute as they said you were." Coast gave me a wink and stepped back so we could enter the building. "Atlas said he wanted to teach you how to skate."

"Did he?" I looked at Atlas sidelong.

Atlas grinned. "I did. Coast was nice enough to say we could use the ice for an hour or two."

"That's not how I remember the conversation going," Coast said. "I recall bribery and maybe a threat or two."

"Your memory is failing you, Riggs," Atlas said. "For the record, I offered no bribes or threats."

"This time," Jay said.

"I like to keep my options open," Atlas said, grinning.

"I like to think you're smarter than to actually try to threaten me," Coast said sweetly. He turned to me and added, "Atlas knows how easy it would be for me to make him disappear. Lucky for both of us, he's harmless, for the most part."

He reminded me of Frost. Smiling and friendly on the outside, dangerous as hell on the inside. He was also a valued employee of the Brantley family.

Formerly centre for the Dusk Bay Demons, he retired a couple of years ago, but stuck around to coach and do jobs for his boss on the side. Rumour had it, he once killed a man with his ice skate. I had no idea if that was true or not, but this was Dusk Bay; nothing would surprise me.

Plus, they don't call them knife shoes for nothing.

Atlas rolled his eyes. "That's what I want everyone to think."

Jay patted his bicep. "We really know you're not harmless. Right Chelsea?"

I looked at all of them, opened my mouth, then closed it again. Slowly shook my head and said, "You said something about skating?"

Coast chuckled. "I like this woman. I might have to introduce you to Sinclair, my girlfriend. I think you two would get along." He closed the door behind us and waved us toward a nearby corridor.

Chapter Twenty

Chelsea

"THAT WAS AMAZING!" I SAT DOWN IN THE locker room to untie the laces of my skates. "I didn't even fall on my ass once."

"That's because I was behind you the entire time, ready to catch you," Atlas pointed out.

"Yes, you were." I looked up at him and smiled.

He sat on a bench beside Jay, who already had his skates off and was wriggling his bare toes in relief. He hadn't seemed uncomfortable while skating, but he was definitely happier out of the confining footwear.

"I wasn't going to let anything happen to you," Atlas said. "If you're going to have bruises on your ass, I want to be the one who puts them there, not from you falling."

"What he said," Jay agreed.

"You guys say the sweetest things," I said. "Who else would think to say stuff like that?"

"Frost?" Jay suggested.

"Okay, he would," I said. "So would Dallas, I guess. Storm would enjoy bruises on my ass, regardless of how they got there."

"I knew he was a sadistic prick," Atlas said. "That confirms it."

"He's not so much sadistic as..." I didn't know how to finish that sentence.

"Sadistic," Atlas finished for me. It's okay, you don't need to cover for him. We know what he's like, don't we Jay?"

Jay shrugged. "Maybe we do and maybe we don't. I guess we'll find out. He's accepted that we're going to hang around, right?"

"He has," I agreed. "He's been kind enough to give you his permission to spend time with me, remember?"

Both of them snorted.

"He's all heart," Atlas said sarcastically. "And all cock. As in, he's a cockhead."

"I knew that was what you were trying to say," I said. Should I tell them about the bet between Frost and Dallas? The one about Storm and Atlas being friends someday? They'd probably find it funny, but Atlas might find it a challenge. He might decide not to be friendly with Storm, so Frost would lose. What would he have to gain by doing that though? Maybe I'd tell them later.

"I thought you might," Atlas said, breaking through my thoughts. "You're a smart woman and it's pretty obvious Storm Keller is a cockhead."

I rolled my eyes at him. "I promise you, Storm isn't that bad when you get to know him. And when he gets to know you. When he does, he'll let up and let you in."

"Can we not talk about him anymore?" Atlas asked. "We were having fun but that doesn't need to stop." He cocked his head at me in a meaningful, suggestive way.

I glanced around us. "Here? What if Coast came back in and found us?"

A shiver of excitement passed through me. I wasn't shy about fucking in front of other people, or getting caught. Not unless the person who caught us had loose lips. That was a rumour I didn't need to get around town. It wouldn't be a good look for me or the team.

Atlas gestured dismissively with his hand. "Coast

is long gone by now. He let us in, but he told me to let ourselves out. The only people left in the arena are us and a few cleaners and security."

"What if *they* walk in on us?" I asked, no more deterred by that than by the idea of being busted by Coast.

"Then they might learn a thing or two," Atlas said. " I bet we could show them things they never dreamed of."

"Or fantasised about," Jay agreed.

Atlas pointed a finger gun at him. "That too. We could give them something for their spank bank."

"When you put it that way." I pushed myself up off the seat and stood in front of them both. I glanced at Atlas, then at Jay.

"Would you dance for us?" Jay asked. "Like you used to at Flirts?" His tongue slid over his lips like he wasn't sure if he asked for too much.

I smiled. "Of course I will." I loved to dance. I always would. Just because I didn't do it in front of a room full of men anymore, didn't mean I wouldn't do it for the guys I cared about. I'd already done it for the other three, why not for these two? I briefly wondered if Ramsey would want me to strip for him too. Did he know what I used to do for a living?

Since he was apparently more deeply embedded in the culture of Dusk Bay than I previously suspected, I expected he did. I got the distinct impression he knew a *lot* more than he let on.

Putting him out of my mind for now, I started to sway to music only I could hear. A beat in my mind and a melody danced to a million times before.

I ran my hands up and down my body, over my stomach and up to my breasts. Slowly, I started to work loose the buttons of my blouse. One by one, giving them a hint of skin, then a little more.

Both guys watched avidly, their eyes wide and fixed on me. The tents in their pants growing by the moment. Pushing at the fabric, threatening to burst the seams.

I undid the bottom button of my blouse and turned my back on them to slide it down my shoulders and onto the chair I'd been sitting on. Glancing over my shoulder at them, I unhooked my bra and let it slide down my arms and land on top of the blouse.

Without turning back to them, I undid my jeans and pushed them down my hips before stepping out of them. I wiggled my ass at them and pushed my panties down to kick them aside.

I raised my arms above my head and lowered

them slowly to grip my ankles. Giving them a full view of my rear hole.

"Holy fuck," Atlas breathed.

"You said it," Jay agreed. "Chelsea, you're incredible. So fucking amazing."

My head still down, I smiled at them from between my legs before straightening back up. I'd have to keep practising, or I'd lose my flexibility. That would suck, to say the least.

Atlas held out his hand. He pulled me to him when I took it and drew me closer until I stood between his legs.

"Jay is right, you're incredible. So fucking hot." He pulled me down to his knee and slammed his mouth down onto mine. His tongue explored inside my mouth, while his and Jay's hands wandered over my body.

I lay back across their legs, letting them see all of me and touch me however they wanted to. Wherever they wanted to.

Both feasted on me with their eyes, before rolling and pinching my nipples and sliding their hands between my legs.

"She's so wet," Jay marvelled, sliding his fingers up and down my slit.

"She's wet for us," Atlas said. "What do you think we should do with that?" He glanced at me speculatively.

"Whatever you want," I said. "Tell me."

I'd played out this scenario before with clients, but this was different. It wasn't just about fulfilling the needs of a paying customer. This was about giving pleasure to two men I cared about, and receiving it back from them. It was about giving them the freedom to show me how they liked to fuck.

"I want you to fuck Jay," Atlas said. "He hasn't had the pleasure of your pussy yet. I want to see him take you."

Jay swallowed audibly. "I want that too. Please."

He was so sweet to ask nicely.

I pushed myself up off them and knelt in front of Jay. I undid the buttons of his jeans and pulled back the flaps of denim. His boxer shorts were next. I hooked my pointer fingers in the waistband and pulled them down to let his erection spring free.

He lifted his hips to push his pants and boxers down to the floor before kicking them aside.

I climbed onto his lap, straddling his thighs and gripping his shoulders. My eyes on his, I lowered myself down onto his cock. Slowly, slowly, bit by bit, easing and deeper and deeper inside me.

His breath caught in the back of his throat. "Fucking hell. You feel so good." He grabbed the hem of his shirt and pulled it over his head before tossing it aside.

"You look good together," Atlas said. "Talk about material for a spank bank." He pushed down the front of his jeans and gripped his cock in one hand.

Jay looked at him uncertainly. "You shouldn't have to—"

Atlas waved him off. "Enjoy yourself. Fuck our woman and let me watch. I'm here for it."

My hands still on his shoulders, I pushed myself up until my pussy almost slid off Jay's cock. Faster than before, I lowered myself back down. Again and again, I rode his lap, my breasts bouncing with each movement.

Jay watched them before cupping them, palming my nipples and rubbing his rough skin against them. The friction was incredible. Perfection.

Between that and the way Atlas pumped himself, his eyes glued to us, I was on the edge of orgasm in a handful of minutes.

The idea someone might walk in at any moment didn't hurt either. I was hoping they would. Let them see. Let them stand there and watch. In my fantasy, they joined in as well, but unless it was one of my guys, that wouldn't happen. I was a five-and-a-half man, woman. Six if Ramsey joined our little crew.

I pictured him standing in the doorway, watching. Stepping over to me and pushing his pants down to slide his cock into my mouth. I'd suck him hard harder than he'd ever been sucked before. Right before he pulled out of my mouth and came all over my face and hair.

That thought had me coming so hard, my release gushed out of me, all over Jay's cock and lap.

"Holy—" Then Jay came too. Thrusting frantically up into me as he spilled himself inside me, his release mingling with mine. He ground himself against me hard, drawing out both of our orgasms for as long as he could.

I'd just started to catch my breath when Atlas stood and pressed his cock between my lips the way Ramsey did in my fantasy.

"You looked hungry," he remarked.

I looked up at him with smiling eyes and sucked, one hand on his balls, the other still on Jay's shoulder. His cock still inside me.

Atlas thrust a couple of times, fucking my mouth right there in the arena locker room without a care in the world. His hips swayed with each thrust, driving him deep each time and making me gag, but neither of us pulled away. Not until he came, squirting salty, delicious cum into my mouth.

I pulled my lips off his cock with a pop and pressed them to Jay's. When he opened his mouth, I let the cum trickle inside.

He smiled and gestured for Atlas to lower his mouth to his, passing the cum back to the big inside centre.

Atlas swished it around in his mouth a few times before lowering his mouth to mine and giving it back.

I made a sound of appreciation in the back of my throat and swallowed it all down. Every delicious drop.

"No wonder the other guys are obsessed with you," Jay said. "I think I am too."

"I *know* I am," Atlas said. "I'm obsessed with both of you. Neither of you are getting rid of me now. You're both mine and I'm yours."

"All yours,"Jay agreed.

They made it sound so simple, all I could do was smile. And hope like hell, things didn't get any more complicated.

"We should go," I said. "We should definitely do this again. Maybe with the other guys next time. "

"Maybe," Atlas said with a shrug. "One step at a time."

"Yeah, one step at a time," I said softly.

There were other things I needed to take care of first. Like making sure my brother knew not to mess with any of my guys. That might be easier said than done.

Chapter Twenty One

Chelsea

"It's been so long since both of you were here for dinner." Mum didn't bother to hide her delight. "I can't remember the last time the four of us sat down together."

"It was about four months ago," I said. I sat down on the couch next to my brother and placed my phone on the coffee table in front of me, Screen down, like always. When I was here, I was always as present as I could be.

Mum frowned. "It feels longer than that. Anyway, make yourself comfortable. The spaghetti will be ready soon."

"My favourite." Ice rubbed his stomach.

"That's why I made it." She happily disappeared into the kitchen, leaving us alone in the living room.

"I keep trying to convince her to move in with me so I can eat home-cooked meals every day," Ice remarked. He laced his hands behind his head and leaned back against the couch.

"Are you trying to tell me there's four of you living in that house and none cook?" I teased.

"Oh, we cook, but Mum's cooking is better than ours. That's why we all love coming here to eat." He propped his feet on the coffee table. "They'd be here tonight, but Mannix had a thing, and took Kennedy and Ares with him."

I eyed him, only the fact he wasn't wearing shoes kept me from scolding him. If Dad saw him with his feet on the table, he'd have something to say.

"When are you bringing your boyfriends to dinner?" he continued.

Sometimes we had dinner with my brother and his partners and sometimes it was just the four of us. Mum liked cooking for us either way, but it was nice to catch up without the crowd.

"I don't know," I said. "Right now, if I brought them here, it might end up in a food fight."

"You say 'food fight' like it's a bad thing." He grinned.

"It is if it involves bludgeoning someone with a

leg of lamb," I said dryly. "Mum wouldn't be impressed if they wasted food like that."

Ice chuckled. "Trouble in paradise? Did you figure things out with Atlas?" Finally he got down to what he really wanted to ask.

I told him everything Atlas and Daze told me, including how happy she was that she'd found a way to get me back into the fold.

Ice looked just as happy.

"I told you, you couldn't stay away for long." He reached over to pat my knee.

"If you say 'welcome to the dark side,' I'm going to be the one bludgeoning you with a leg of lamb," I warned.

He grinned. "That's my baby sister. Threatening people with roasted farm animals. You'll be threatening to shoot me next."

"You don't have to look so happy about it," I said. "This wasn't what I wanted for my life."

I would have settled for the guys understanding the way Dusk Bay worked, and who to be wary of. I'd never intended for them to become minions of the Brantley family. I certainly never intended to get personally involved. I could kick myself for it now.

He scooted over closer, put an arm around me and pulled me to him. "I know it wasn't, but did you really think you could avoid it forever? Even if you left Dusk Bay, Dusk Bay wouldn't leave you. Sooner or later, they would have found a way to get you to do what they want."

"You're okay with that?" I nestled up against him, enjoying the feeling of safety he always gave me.

The guys said they'd kill for me, but my brother would go further than that. He'd burn the world down for the people he loved. Tear it apart and leave it in ashes.

"I'm not happy that you're not happy," he said. "But I know you will be. You have...how many guys into you?"

I swallowed. "Six," I admitted. "Well, five and a half, but close enough."

He laughed into my hair. "Six? That's my baby sister. A badass doctor with six boyfriends. All six of them better make sure they take care of you. Other-wise, they'll have me to answer to."

"They wouldn't dare to piss you off," I said. "Frost seems to idolise you. He'd probably want to help eviscerate the other five."

"I've been thinking about taking on an appren-tice," Ice said thoughtfully. "Any other likely recruits?"

"To your skillset? I don't think so. Storm would

prefer to break fingers. Atlas too. They have more in common than they realise."

"We can never have too many hired thugs," Ice said. "What about the others?"

"Jay and Dallas seem happy to go with the flow," I said slowly. "Although, Jay is given to pranking people. I get the impression he's good at not getting caught."

"An interesting skill set," Ice said. "Once in a while, pranks turn deadly."

"That sounds like a television show," I said. I made my voice sound like a TV presenter. "*When pranks go wrong.*"

Ice laughed. "I'd watch."

"That doesn't surprise me," I said. "As for Ramsey, Daze said we're taking orders from him. I don't think Storm or Atlas are too happy about that. Storm in particular. He might push back."

"From what I've seen of him, I'd expect nothing less," Ice mused. "I'm sure they'll work it out. Hopefully without bloodshed."

I sat up a little and stared at him. "Did you just say you hoped there wasn't bloodshed?" I pressed a hand to his forehead. "You don't feel hot."

"I don't *always* want blood spilled." He grabbed my wrist and pulled my hand down to his chest.

"Who are you and what have you done with my brother?" I asked. "Because the one I know would write a book about a hundred ways to make someone bleed while killing them slowly."

"One hundred and one," he said. "I could probably come up with a series of books, if I'm honest. But you care about these guys and you don't want them to kill each other, right? And you're my sister, so I want what you want. If you don't want them spilling each other's blood, they better not."

"If you're about to say you'll spill their blood if they spill each other's blood, I'm not sure it works that way." I sat back against him again.

This whole conversation was starting to make my head spin, like we were going around in circles. Threats of violence to prevent threats of violence. Blood after blood.

We were definitely *not* normal people.

"I have other methods," he said. "I've been working on how to cause pain without breaking the skin. It's fascinating. You should come down to my work room sometime. Let me show you what I've been working on."

"On the face of the planet, only you would say something like that," I said.

If I was fascinated with pain the way he was, I

only had to turn up at work on any given day. There was always someone injured, or recovering from an injury.

I was definitely *not* going to admit that one thing I liked about the job was exactly that. Seeing the guys throw themselves into the game until they were battered, bruised and sometimes with broken bones. I definitely didn't get off on that, no way.

"Only me?" he mused. "Probably not, but I like to be unique. How boring would life be if we were all the same?"

"That's what I keep trying to say," I said. "I was quite happy living my life away from all the violence. Just to be different, you know?"

"Poor Chels." He kissed my forehead. "You'll do fine. Did you know Daisy Lasalle got out for a few years? She thought she put it behind her, but look at her now. She's just about running this city. And loving every moment of it. Once she embraced her true self, she really started living."

"I'm not like her," I said.

"Aren't you?" he asked. "If you weren't, you wouldn't have brought Belinda Simmons to me. But you did. A person living a normal life would have— Actually, I don't know what they would have done.

Letting someone like that ruin your life seems like a bad idea to me."

"You think?" I asked with a hint of sarcasm. I closed my eyes and sighed slowly. "I didn't know what else to do. I would have been kicked out of the Smashers if Bruce knew sooner than he did. I wouldn't have been able to finish my practical placement, much less got a job with the team. She would have destroyed everything."

"So you did what you had to do and destroyed her first," he concluded.

"I'm still not like Daze," I argued.

I didn't get a kick out of controlling people the way she seemed to. I didn't want people scared of me. At least, not consciously.

Also not something I'd admit to myself.

Although, maybe that was why I didn't mind the guys giving me the occasional roofie, or acting out a kidnapping and being rough with me. If I relinquished power to them, maybe it would stop me from going after it myself.

Possibly, deep down, I craved it a lot more than I realised.

"Do you regret bringing Belinda to me?" he asked.

I chewed my lip for a few moments before finally

responding. "Not exactly. I asked her not to publish that story and she wouldn't listen. I gave her a choice. She decided screwing with my life was perfectly okay. I wish she'd done what I asked. We both could have walked away."

I couldn't bring myself to admit, even to myself, that I enjoyed the fear in her eyes. If I accepted that fact, I was one step deeper into what seemed to me like a dark, black hole. One I'd been skirting around for years, but managed to avoid falling into. Like a black hole in space, it was difficult to resist its pull. If I didn't keep trying, I could disappear inside forever. Losing myself and everything I spent so long working towards.

My brother would tell me to embrace it, but I couldn't. I'd keep fighting until I had no fight left in me.

"You really think she would have?" He squeezed my shoulders. "People like her are always looking for an angle. If it wasn't that article, on that day, it would have been another. It might have been something with even bigger fallout. And it might have come at a time when you were too late to stop it. Like you said, you gave her a choice and she made it. People don't always make good choices. That other dancer, what was her name? Ivy? She also made choices. So did Bruce Fergus. Every single day I get out of bed and I have to make choices and live with them. That was exactly what they did. But their choices killed them instead. It's not your fault they had bad intentions and bad reasoning. All we can do is our best in life and look out for the people we love."

"You're right," I said slowly.

"I'm your big brother, I'm always right," he said with a laugh. "It's my job. Autopsies, torture and wisdom. Huh, I should get that on a T-shirt."

"And one that says 'I kill people and I know things,'" I said dryly.

"That would be perfect." He laughed again. "Although, it might raise some eyebrows. Nothing says 'subtle' like a T-shirt like that."

"On the other hand, no one would suspect anyone would wear that on a T-shirt if they really did it," I pointed out. "It might be the perfect disguise, out in the open."

"Now you're the wise one," he said. "I'll look into that. Would you like one?"

"I think I'll pass," I said. I opened my mouth to add something, but Mum called out first.

"Kids, dinner is ready!"

"Perfect, I'm starving." He tugged me to my feet and pushed me towards the dining table, laughing like we were children again.

Chapter Twenty Two

Dallas

"How is the knee?"

"A little stiff."

I stopped out of sight of the doorway leading into the infirmary. I shouldn't listen in on another player's medical appointment, but I recognised both of those voices. Doctor Otis Skinner and Ramsey. Why would Ramsey see Skinner if he could see Chelsea?

I frowned, and went on listening.

"Have you been doing the exercises I instructed you to do?" Skinner asked. "They should help to ease the stiffness."

I grimaced. I wished they'd stop using that word. I'd come to see Chelsea because of a stiffness problem of my own. One that was rapidly deflating.

"Yeah, but it's still stiff," Ramsey said. "I've been putting extra time in, but I was thinking I could do more pool work. If it doesn't start to loosen up, it could put my season at risk."

Skinner clicked his tongue. "Wouldn't want that."

"Definitely not." Ramsey seemed unimpressed by his response.

Feeling like the mafia spy we joked about, I took a step forward and peered around the doorway.

Both men stood with their backs to the door. Otis Skinner's body was as tense as ever, but Ramsey looked relaxed. Like this man posed no threat to him in any way. Either he was a great actor, or he was up to something.

I couldn't rule out the possibility I was getting paranoid after everything I learned in the last couple of months. My gut told me otherwise. Something was up and I needed to stick around and listen, and not be seen.

I ducked back into the corridor and leaned against the wall. Silently, I pulled my phone out of my pocket and started to record the conversation.

"We can certainly have you do more exercises," Skinner said. "I've run through the ones your physical therapist recommended. I can add to that. And book you in for more time in the pool. You do significant aqua therapy in the off-season, correct?"

"Yeah, Never feels like enough," Ramsey said. "I could stay there all day."

"There is such a thing as over exercising," Skinner warned. "If you put too much strain on your body, or lose too much weight, it will have an adverse affect on you and your playing."

Now he mentioned it, I had noticed Ramsey working out more than the rest of us. Which was saying something, since we spent a shit load of time exercising.

Over exercising was something we all had to watch out for. Obsessing over food, weight and body image in general was dangerous for anyone, and a trap too easy for people like us to fall into. It could become an unhealthy obsession without us realising it.

"I'm aware," Ramsey said. "I still need my knee right."

"Yes, the long-term impacts could be adverse if we don't address them now," Skinner said. "Not to mention it might interfere with other plans."

"Not going to interfere," Ramsey argued.

"If you're sidelined, or sent to another team, it

might," Skinner said. "Timing is everything. As I'm sure you're well aware."

"Yep," Ramsey said. That one simple word conveyed a great deal of irritation. Like he didn't appreciate the doctor telling him what to do, even if it was a professional opinion.

Meanwhile, I wondered what the hell they were talking about. Did this have anything to do with Dominic King? Was it possible Ramsey was working for him and not with us? If he was, a stiff knee would be the least of his problems.

I leaned closer as one of them stepped further away, holding my phone out so I wouldn't miss anything. I had my eyes on the screen, so if anyone walked past they'd just think I stopped to doom scroll. I wouldn't be the first person distracted by social media in the middle of a corridor.

"Is everything in place?" Skinner asked.

"Almost," Ramsey replied. "Couple of things to sort out."

Skinner clicked his tongue. "There's always something. Or someone."

Footsteps clicked on the floor, closer to the doorway.

I pressed on a random social media and

engrossed myself in the latest Booktok trend. It was about time they noticed rugby players' thighs.

The footsteps moved away, deeper into the room again.

"What's left?" Skinner asked.

"Nothing major," Ramsey said.

"Care to elaborate?" Skinner sounded increasingly irritated. Either with plans not going the way he wanted, or with Ramsey's short responses.

"Not in the loop enough?" Ramsey asked, his tone goading.

"I should be the loop," Skinner snapped.

Ramsey snorted derisively. "Don't get ahead of yourself. You're just part of the loop."

"For now," Skinner said. "After this, that will change. They'll sit up and take notice."

"Won't be able to," Ramsey said.

Skinner barked a short laugh. "That's true. They'll be dealt with and we'll be in a better position than we already were."

I pictured him rubbing his hands together like a cartoon villain. Did he have a fluffy white cat and a lair?

Once, I would have thought that was just stuff that only happened in the movies. Now I wasn't so sure. I'd seen a lot of strange things recently. Things I wouldn't have ever expected to see. Things that were both exciting and terrifying at the same time. Much more terrifying than a cat and a cave.

Depending on the cat.

Speaking of positions, where was Chelsea? I assumed she wasn't in the infirmary, or they wouldn't be talking like this. The things they said, you didn't say in front of witnesses. If they knew they had any. Was it possible they knew I was out here? I didn't think so. If they did, they'd be more careful.

"If it works," Ramsey said. "Don't assume."

"I'd never assume," Skinner said. "I don't need to. We know what needs to be done and how to execute it. Everything will happen flawlessly."

I winced at his choice of words. Did they mean it literally? Who was the 'they,' Ramsey and Skinner were talking about? Was it us? Me and Chelsea's other boyfriends?

Was Ramsey plotting against us? This was a damning conversation if he was. It sounded to me like he was planning to double cross all of us. Whoever decided we were supposed to take orders from him must have badly misjudged his loyalty.

I stared at my phone screen without seeing anything. I didn't want to think Ramsey was working against us. If he was, I'd misjudged him too. I thought he was a decent guy. One I would have shared Chelsea with.

If they were saying what they *seemed* to be saying, then I wouldn't let him anywhere near her. How was I supposed to do that? I didn't know, but if he was planning against us, then I'd do whatever I had to do.

"It better," Ramsey said. "I've put everything in this. If this doesn't work, I'm screwed."

Skinner responded with a nasty sounding chuckle. "You won't be the only one screwed. Although, screwed will be the least of our problems. Dead is more likely."

"I'm not easy to kill," Ramsey declared.

"They all say that until they're proven wrong," Skinner said. "We all have weaknesses. Even myself."

"Yeah?" Ramsey asked. It didn't sound as though he expected an answer, but he couldn't resist asking anyway. Maybe he'd get one.

Just in case, I listened carefully. Anything we could learn about Otis Skinner could be valuable information in the future. Potentially, not even the distant future.

Skinner snorted. "I don't trust you enough to give you that information, Ferris."

They were on first name terms now? I didn't

know anyone who referred to Ramsey by his first name. It was always Ramsey, Ram, or Goat. What did it mean that Skinner called him Ferris?

"You should trust me," Ramsey said. "I'm the one putting shit in place. I mess up, you're fucked."

"Don't mess up," Skinner warned. "You won't like the consequences if you screw up and we don't, somehow, end up dead."

"Don't threaten me," Ramsey said. "I might fuck up on purpose."

I couldn't see his eyes, but I imagined them narrowing with irritation. Violence burning just under the surface. Ready to lash out without notice.

"It'll be the last thing you do," Skinner said.

"I said, don't threaten me," Ramsey growled. "It'll be the last thing *you* do."

They definitely weren't best friends. Presumably they didn't need to be, to pull off whatever it was they planned.

If I didn't know better, I'd think they didn't like each other. Like Storm and Atlas, they were thrown together. If that was the case, who did the throwing? Was it Dominic King? If it wasn't him, then who? I'd bet a season's earnings they weren't working for the Brantley family.

At least, Otis Skinner wasn't. There was no

doubt in my mind of that. The doctor gave me the creeps. I always got the impression he knew exactly what was going on right under the first layer of my skin. Not in a medical way, but in a way that saw into me, peeling those layers back and worming into places he shouldn't be.

I didn't trust him as far as I could spit. Even before Atlas said he wasn't to be trusted, I didn't.

Ramsey— I still didn't want to believe he was working against us. If he was, they could go on threatening each other as much as they wanted to. If they were the enemy and they took each other out, that would save us all a lot of hassle.

Okay, I was new to this mafia shit, but I knew it wouldn't be that easy. We couldn't just sit back and wait for the trash to take itself out. Nope, I'd have to tell Chelsea, and the other guys about this and see what we'd be ordered to do.

Was there any chance we'd be told to kill Ramsey? I shook my head and scrolled past another video. If it came to that, I'd do what was necessary, but I wouldn't like it. He was my teammate. I thought he was my friend.

Fuck. Conflict swirled around in my brain.

"Just get things in place," Skinner snapped. "We're running out of time to do this. If we don't act soon, it'll be too late. Then both our heads will be on the chopping block. Possibly literally. I'm fucked if I'm going to let that happen."

"Stop being twitchy," Ramsey told him. "They said you always keep calm."

Who were they? I screwed up my face, hoping he'd elaborate, but he didn't.

"I do," Skinner said coldly. "I'm not being twitchy, I'm being cautious. Something I've come to expect from all of the people I work with. If you can't do that, I'll ask for someone else."

Ramsey laugh-grunted. "They won't give you someone else. You have the best. Be calm."

"I'm perfectly calm," Skinner said. "If a touch impatient." He sounded like Storm, ready to talk off body parts and use them as blunt instruments.

I couldn't imagine him doing that. He seemed more contained. More likely to slide a quiet blade between someone's ribs, or something like that. Not hands-on and messy.

Footsteps moved closer to the door again.

I took a few back, eyes still on my phone screen. I hadn't really watched the last four or five videos, but the couple of people who walked past me didn't give me a second glance. None stopped to wonder what was going on inside the infirmary. They didn't so much as hesitate.

The footsteps stopped right inside the doorway.

I glanced up as Ramsey looked out, right at me.

He didn't look surprised to see me. He raised an eyebrow. "Heard enough?"

Shit.

Chapter Twenty Three

Dallas

Sʜɪᴛ!

Chapter Twenty Four

Chelsea

"Don't fall in love with any," Storm warned Frost. "We're not taking any of them home."

Frost smiled and gestured around the array of cages that made up the pet rescue.

"How can I not fall in love with any of them? For that matter, *all* of them? Look at that one for example." He pointed towards a blue heeler, who sat looking back at us, her tail thumping on the ground. "Don't tell me you can resist that face." He gave Storm his own version of puppy dog eyes.

"My apartment is not made for dogs," Storm said. "We're here for the press, remember? So we can look like good guys who love little animals."

"We are good guys who love little animals," Frost said. He crouched down in front of the blue heeler's cage and started talking to her in a low, soothing voice.

"Still not taking any home," Storm muttered.

"We might need that mansion." I wound my arm through his and stepped over to admire a cage full of kittens.

"Your pussy is the only one I need," he said in my ear.

I turned to whisper back to him. "But they're so cute. That black one looks just like a little panther."

"I already have a panther," he whispered meaningfully. "And if you keep pushing me, she's going to be a punished panther."

"That won't help your good guy image," I teased.

"Good." He cocked his head and made a face at the kitten. He might have softened slightly.

"They want us over there," Atlas said.

When I turned around, he jerked his head towards the camera crew. I unwound myself from Storm and stepped back, out of the way. This was about the guys, not me. Generating good publicity for the team. What could be better than filming them cuddling puppies?

I scanned the handful of people who stood around. Other guys from the team, a handful of staff and volunteers from the shelter. I saw no sign of

Dallas. Ramsey arrived a few minutes late, but Dallas should have been here by now.

I pulled out my phone and pressed on his number before putting the device to my ear.

The call went straight to voicemail. No doubt, he was on his way and I was worrying for nothing. Still, I stepped over to Ramsey.

"Hey, you didn't see Dallas on your way here?" I asked.

"I saw him at the stadium," Ramsey said. "He left before me. He's not here?" He glanced around.

"I'm sure he'll be here soon," I said. "It's not like him to be late." If anything, he was usually early. Especially if he knew he could be alone with me for a while. In this case, he was missing puppies.

"Yeah," Ramsey agreed. He didn't seem particularly worried.

If he wasn't, I guessed I could take my cue from him.

In spite of that, I felt uneasy. While the guys were handed puppies to cuddle, I stepped out to look up and down the road. The stadium loomed over the city in the distance, traffic flowed between there and here.

"He's probably caught in traffic," I told myself. Which didn't explain why he wasn't here if he left before Ramsey. I tried his phone again, but once again, it went to voicemail. Even if he was driving, he could have answered, couldn't he?

"I have a bad feeling about this," I whispered to myself. Something wasn't adding up. It was giving me chills up and down my spine.

I headed back inside. I'd ask Ramsey exactly where he saw Dallas last. Maybe Dallas got sidetracked with something and hadn't left the stadium when Ramsey thought he had.

I tucked my phone into my back pocket and stopped to look at Ramsey looking back at me. Something in his gaze made me freeze on the spot.

What had he done?

Thank you for reading! The story continues in Bad Ruck. For a lighter, bonus scene with Chelsea and Sadie, you can download that here.

About the Author

Maggie Alabaster writes reverse harem romance.

She lives in NSW, Australia with one spouse, two daughters, one dog, and countless birds.

Sign up for Maggie's newsletter! Sign Up!

Join Maggie's reader group! Join here!

Follow Maggie on Bookbub! Click here to follow me!

Check out Maggie's website- www.maggiealabaster.com

Also by Maggie Alabaster

Ruck Boys

Filthy Ruck

Hard Ruck

Twisted Ruck

Bad Ruck

Dirty Ruck

Deadly Ruck

Sparrow and the Mafia Kings

Possessive

Ruined

Corrupted

Pucking Dark Hearts

Pucking Hearts Collide

Pucking Forbidden Hearts

Pucking Hardened Hearts

Dusk Bay Demons

Puck Drop

Breakaway

Power Play

Brutal Academy

Book 1 Heartless

Book 2 Cruel

Book 3 Vengeful

Court of Blood and Binding

Book 1 Song of Scent and Magic

Book 2 Crown of Mist and Heat

Book 3 Sword of Balm and Shadow

Book 4 Whisper of Frost and Flame

Dark Masque

Book 1 Bait

Book 2 Prey

Book 3 Trap

Saving Abbie

Book 1 Pitch

Book 2 Pound

Book 3 Session

Book 4 Muse

Book 5 Rhythm

Book 6 Encore

Novella Venomous

Saving Abbie books 1-4

Saving Abbie books 4-6 + Venomous

Ruthless Claws

Book 1 Ivory

Book 2 Crimson

Book 3 Elodie

Harmony's Magic

Book 1 Summoned by Fire

Book 2 Summoned by Fate

Book 3 Summoned by Desire

Shifter's Vault

Book 1 Discarded

Book 2 Deceived

Book 3 Disgraced

My Alien Mates

Book 1 Star Warriors

Book 2 Star Defenders

Book 3 Star Protectors

Academy of Modern Magic

Book 1 Digital Magic

Book 2 Virtual Magic

Book 3 Logical Magic

Complete Collection

Summer's Harem

Book 1: Shimmer

Book 2: Glimmer

Book 3: Flicker

Complete collection

Short reads

Taken by the Snowmen

Jingle All the Way

Also by Maggie Alabaster and Erin Yoshikawa

Caught by the Tide

Book 1—Pursued by Shadows

Book 2 Pursued by Darkness

Book 3 Pursued by Monsters